Beyond the Sunset

A Novel by

George G. Brainard

This novel is loosely based on the grief experiences of the author. Some of the characters, places and events are strictly fictitious others are based loosely on reality as the author remembers it. For details please see "Clarifications – To Set the Record Straight" located on pages 239-242.

First edition, first printing

ISBN 978-0-9914498-0-4 softcover

Library of Congress Catalog Card Number – pending

Published by

George G. Brainard
PO Box 508
Belmont, Michigan 49306-0508

Printed by

Dickinson Press
5100 33rd Street SE
Grand Rapids, Michigan 49512

Printed in the United States of America

Dedication

This book is humbly and lovingly presented in memory of my lover, wife and soul mate for 44 plus years –

Louise Jane Brainard

Thanks to those who read as I wrote – offering advice and encouragement along the way (listed alphabetically)

Marinus Bazen – Cheryl Dalton – Cathy Ditmar – Gary & Beth Evanzo – Mary Good – Doug & Donna Hansen Toni Hecksel – Sandy Herrema – Malia Hurley – Kendal Lentz – Geof & Cindy Livezey – Joyce Maczka – Lori Noorman – Gerald Painter – Judy Pearson – Mike & Sandi Richman – Tom Rohrer – David & Carol Torgerson – Dana Tosh – Carolyn VanBemden

Special thanks to those who assisted me with editing and publishing

Karen Brainard – Geof Livezey – Tedd Litty

and

My friends at Dickinson Press

Dear Reader,

You may be asking yourself...

"Why should I read this book?"

That's a good question. Let me tell you why I wrote it.

A line that agents and editors frequently hear goes something like this: "God gave me this book and it needs to be published so that everyone can read it and be changed." I have no such illusion about my writing.

God has already given us His Book – we call it the Holy Bible. He had the profound wisdom to inspire dozens of writers over several centuries to give us His revelation. It shows us who He is, who we are, and His plans for us. This Bible has been:

Analyzed ... Berated
Criticized ... Debated
Eulogized ... Fabricated
Glamorized ... Hated
and so much more.

God's Word stands, and has completely changed the lives of countless individuals who have taken the time to read it with an open mind and willing heart. So, NO! God doesn't need my help.

That being said, my little book comes from a concern I've had for several years. One you may have had as well. Over those years I have encountered a number of folk who have talked about a faith they once had but now show no interest whatsoever. What happened? How did this disconnect come about? Many times we hear, "God – if there is a God – has let me down."

My wife, Jane, and I frequently discussed people we knew – friends and family – who had "left the faith." That is, if they ever were "in the faith." We talked about, someday, writing a story dealing on this troubling matter. We agreed that a life-shaking tragedy would be needed to bring our main character to their point of doubt and rejection. I suggested the tragic loss of a loved one – like a son in the military or a child in an accident. I had no idea that I would lose my own dear wife to a massive heart attack on January 19, 2009 – a few weeks before her sixty-third birthday. Suddenly, I was plunged into the challenges our main character was to experience.

Understandably, I was in no position to start writing very soon. Three years later, I started collecting my thoughts and decided it was time to write my book. Yes, parts of it are my own story – but I had to exercise my imagination and creativity. So, I guess you would call it a nonfiction novel or faction – that is fact based fiction. Names, personalities and occupations have been changed to suit the plot. Some exaggeration and a few fictitious characters have been added to enhance the overall flavor.

It is my intention and prayer that this book will be a help and blessing to all who are kind enough to read it.

My goal has been to make it a source of:

Comfort to the grieving...
Counsel to the consoling...
Challenge to the doubting...
Caution to the wandering.

Remember – God's Word is our best and final authority.
George G. Brainard ~~~ I Peter 3:15

~ Chapter One ~

As Doctor P. T. (Pete) Daniels shuffled slowly around the university campus, his thoughts drifted ... *The last time Julie and I walked here was almost two years ago ... the day before that horrible night she died so unexpectedly. I wonder if life will ever be ...*

Whoa! Shock waves surged through his body. *What's that in the shadows?* Suddenly he saw what appeared to be a man approaching him and calling out "Mister – oh, mister, can you spare a quarter for some hot coffee?" The pleading voice sounded familiar, but he was still not comfortable with the situation.

As they met under a street light they recognized each other. Pete, whose heart was still racing, said "Oh ... sorry ... did you call me before? I heard a voice but was deep in thought."

"Doctor D., it's you! That explains the deep thought."

"Yes, Jimmy, it's me. What on earth are you doing out here on a cold night like this … where have you been lately?"

Looking down at his feet and avoiding eye contact, he replied "I'm … I'm afraid … that's a long story"

"Well, where can we get that coffee so you can tell me all about it? I've missed you on campus"

Seemingly relieved, he explained that he went to the McDonald's just down the street. They had been good to him the last several weeks – since he lost his job. "I could go to Manny's Café. He gives me free food, but it comes with a lecture and his special brand of spiritual counseling. I'm just not ready for that right now."

"Believe it, or not, I understand. Let's go for that coffee and we can talk. Do you like their pies? I really enjoy the custard pies they are featuring for the holiday season. I bet you're hungry. Order what you want … this one's on me."

They started walking slowly and quietly to McDonald's. When Pete learned that 'just down the street' was over a mile he picked up the pace. Their increased speed prevented any conversation … so neither spoke. The warm restaurant and aroma of fresh hot coffee was a welcome change from the bone chilling Michigan air. Once they had their food and found a seat near the back of the restaurant, Pete broke the silence. "Okay, where do we start?"

Fidgeting with his coffee cup and clearing his throat, Jimmy started nervously. "Well, I came to Grand Valley as a probationary employee. I moved here from out of state where my job was much different from the custodial work I've been doing here."

"I thought you seemed overqualified for your job."

"If … if you only knew" he replied.

"I'm listening." Pete said sensing Jimmy's hesitation.

"How … how much do you want to know?" he asked.

"Tell me as much as you want me to know. I don't have anything else going on tonight. So, let's go - I'm all ears!"

"I'm not sure how far back I should go … I think … I think some of my personal history will help you understand how I got to where I am today."

"Fire away!" Pete replied feeling more like a counselor than a philosophy professor.

Jimmy started "I came from a large, poor family and was the only one able to attend college. My parents couldn't afford to help with the cost, so I had to work. That meant stretching a four year degree out over six years" he said wincing from his obvious embarrassment.

"You needn't be ashamed of that. What was your major? Did you continue your education then? "

This led to a rather lengthy discussion about their college days and the joys and challenges they both experienced.

"Then my father died unexpectedly" he said choking back tears "and I had to help mom support and care for my younger siblings."

"I'm so sorry! Those must have been tough times for you."

"Yes … they were … but we made it!"

"Now then, you had your BA and were back home with family. Did you have any romantic interests at that time?"

"Oh no" he sighed "I didn't have time! I was either working or helping raise a bunch of kids. I was just too busy!"

Pete chuckled "I bet you were. How long did that last?"

"About ten years" he sighed, "until the last two were in their teens and able to fend for themselves."

"I'm sure that gave you some real satisfaction though. How old were you by then?"

"Yes, it did! I was thirty-four – but unencumbered."

"Free to pursue your dreams. Then what?"

"I decided to go for my Master's Degree."

"And …?" Pete prodded.

"I wasn't an honor student, so I had no scholarships, grants or special assistance. I had to work and take classes as time allowed. This took me another five years to earn my Master's Degree. And … I do mean 'earn!' Now I was able to apply for a decent paying job and catch up on my debts."

"Debts?"

"Yes, debts! You see, I had my educational expenses and was continuing to help mom with her expenses. That took another four years but I don't begrudge that. I felt it was my moral obligation."

"Moral?" Pete asked with challenging tone in his voice.

"Well, you know … the right thing to do."

"Yes, I understand. I was just intrigued by your use of the word 'moral' in such a practical situation."

"Is that wrong?" Jimmy replied.

"No. It's just not very often that people see things that way. I think we would all be better off if they did."

"Amen!"

"Amen?" Pete said nervously.

"Yes 'Amen!' Does that offend you? Am I sensing a trend here?"

"No, but the last time I heard that word was in church."

"Are you a 'church going man'?"

"I was …"

"What happened?" Jimmy asked pursuing the subject.

As politely as he could, Pete avoided the matter. "That's a long story. It can wait until our next visit. I'm finding your story most interesting – tell me more."

"Okay … let's see … where were we?"

"You just got a job and were paying off debt."

"Oh, yes ... you're a great listener. You could be a shrink."

If you only knew ... Pete chuckled "Please continue."

"This new job was exactly that – 'a job.' It helped pay off mom's and my bills – but it was not that satisfying. Not what I felt destined to do. Does that make sense to you?"

"Yes but I'm intrigued by your use of the word 'destined'."

"Oh, here we go again. You're 'intrigued' again. Do you intrigue easily?" he chided.

"Maybe I do – but that sounds like more church talk."

"Are you offended by church talk?" he asked sounding somewhat defensive.

"No – but some of your words sound like a familiar voice from the past. A good voice … one I miss dearly." He hesitated briefly – choking away his emotions. "But – that's my story and we can talk about it at another time. We're talking about your story now – let's stay focused. How did you get that elusive satisfaction?"

"I landed a teaching position in a small private school. The pay wasn't that great but it allowed me time to study on the side, so I enrolled in a Doctoral studies program online."

"You must have been in your forties by then, right?"

"Forty-three to be exact. It took four years at 'the job' to find my way clear to further my education. Those were four tough years - but they brought me back to poor but without debt."

"So, now you're forty-three, have a Master's Degree, are teaching and have started your study toward your PhD, correct?"

"Yes. Things were moving toward my big goal – to be Phillip James Simms, PhD. … majoring in Psychology."

"So, your name is Phillip - how did you become just 'Jimmy' the janitor - if I may put it that bluntly?"

"That will have to wait for another time. I see my friends here at Mickey D's are getting ready to close up shop. Thanks for the coffee, pie and listening ears. I've needed to talk with someone like you for some time now."

"Thanks for sharing, Phil. May I call you Phil?"

"Sure, if it's okay to call you Peter." He explained that he knew Pete's full name from reading his bio in some academic journal a few years ago. In recent years Pete has used just his two initials and last name as his signature.

"I prefer Pete – if you don't mind." So they agreed to the less formal names and went their separate ways.

On the way back to his condo, Pete was again deep in thought. However, his contemplation soon shifted from personal quandaries to his conversation with Phil, or as he had known him from campus … Jimmy.

How could a man who seemed to have so much potential be in his present predicament? We do need to spend some more time together – but how? We didn't make any future arrangements - do I just leave it to chance? Was tonight's meeting a 'chance meeting' or part of some strange cosmic plan – unknown to both of us? It was great to have a simple conversation without the sophisticated jargon commonly used by the intellectual crowd. Phil seemed to speak more freely as he opened up and dropped his guard. Hmm ... Two well educated men - just talking as regular guys – none of that 'spectacular vernacular' or 'superficial verbiage' as I often call it. That seemed to show a potential for true friendship. Time will tell. No 'colossal verbosity' ... wow!
Back home, his thoughts continued about Phil and how differently their individual life stories were playing out.

We're both dealing with some serious life struggles – but from vastly different paths. What about all his religious talk? This could be an interesting holiday break ... and it has only begun.

He finally drifted off to sleep with more questions than answers.

~ Chapter Two ~

Pete rolled over and looked at his bedside alarm clock. The large red numbers read 9:07 and he was still in a haze. Christmas break was already having an effect on his sleep habits. He didn't recall having such a restful night in a long time. *Apparently, concentrating on another person's life story is more relaxing than wallowing in my own grief.*

Almost two years had passed since he lost his beloved wife, Julie, and the holidays were some of the hardest times to be alone. *She was my "soul mate." Oh yes, I have family – but the ones who are local are busy with their own families. The others are several hundred miles away – and also very busy. When my family was young, we weren't available that much for my parents either. But, at least, they had each other.*

That's enough self-pity. Now then, what about Phil? It's going to be difficult to start calling him 'Phil' after several months of knowing him as 'Jimmy.' As the chief custodian in Pete's building, he had endeared himself to Pete as a very reliable worker. Frequently, he would leave him notes with special cleaning requests signed simply as 'Dr. D.' He was very impressed with Jimmy's humorous responses. His notes were always written with perfect handwriting and perfect grammar. He was certainly not a typical janitor. This had already piqued Pete's curiosity – but since their meeting last night – he was thoroughly puzzled …
Did he complete his doctoral studies? Had he received his degree? If so, what happened?

He finally hauled himself out of bed - although he wasn't sure why. *I don't have much on my agenda - oh right, what agenda? I'm on vacation - whatever that means. Being alone, unoccupied time is not that enjoyable. Do I need to resurrect some of my old hobbies – or, maybe, start writing another book? My publisher hasn't bothered me lately since my creative juices seem to have run dry.*

As he shaved, showered and went through his morning routine of self-assembly, he thought of things to do to keep busy and ...

Maybe develop some Christmas spirit. I do have my daily obsession with emails and Facebook, something my oldest son set up for me a couple days after Julie passed away. He certainly was right when he said "This will help occupy your time, dad." In the past two years I've acquired over 1500 friends – more than 600 of them were writers. One thing I definitely need to do is meet with Phil – but how? I don't have any contact information.

As he was tossing that dilemma around in his mind, his office phone rang sharply and startled him briefly. He was surprised and pleased to hear Phil's voice.

"Pete? Did I catch you at a bad time?"

"No, Phil, I was just thinking about our conversation last night and wondered how and when we could pick up where we left off. Is there a good time and place for you?"

"So, I didn't bore you with my story? I was hoping we could set up another meeting – an intentional one this time."

Pete still wondered if the first one was really an accident. "Do you have time today?"

Laughing out loud, he replied, “Do I need to remind you that I am unemployed? I have all the time in the world. If you are available, we could meet at McDonald’s again. I do like their dollar menu”

“Great … how does 11:45 sound?”

“Fine, I’ll see you there.”

Pete left right away so he could enjoy an invigorating walk in the crisp, pure Michigan air. Arriving before Phil, he waited in a booth by the door. He was more than a little surprised when he saw him glide into the parking lot on a bicycle – an old one at that. When Phil walked inside, he was wearing the same blue and white GVSU windbreaker as last night. In fact, he appeared to be wearing all the same clothes. At first glance, one might assume that he was a very loyal Lakers fan; but from its obvious wear, this jacket appeared to be his only coat. His facial hair still looked as if untouched for several days – in every way Phil was a mess. At this point, Pete was relieved that he had walked and left his fancy new car in the garage.

After brief greetings, they ordered their food and, took it to their table. Pete asked about the bike and learned that Phil’s car had been repossessed and his budget had been drastically downsized. He was allowed to get out of his apartment lease, and was staying with a friend from his church ... until he could get squared away financially. “When I was suspended without pay, it took a real toll on my lifestyle, Pete. My limited funds, I spend on basic essentials and right here on meals.”

“Suspended? I heard that you were terminated.”

“That’s the story going around campus. Actually, I was suspended pending further investigation.”

"Investigation! For what? This is all news to me."

"Some things were stolen from Dr. Wysocki's office."

"What would they want from a prof's office?"

"I'm told, an expensive laptop computer and a fancy new cell phone were missing when he arrived the next day."

"How did you become a suspect?"

"I found the cell phone in a hallway wastebasket during my early morning cleanup and put it on my desk until I could turn it in to lost and found. Someone must have seen it there and reported it to the campus police. It didn't take long for word to spread about the theft."

"So, did they dust it for fingerprints? You know that all students' prints are on file, right?"

"Yes, I do - and mine were the only prints they found – our thief was no amateur. Because I had been hired on a probationary basis, I became their prime suspect."

"Had you committed a crime during your previous job?"

"Not unless falling asleep on the job is a crime."

"You fell asleep on the job!"

"You've heard about boring lectures, haven't you?

"Of course … I've given some. Were you in one?"

"Worse yet, I was giving one!"

"That is bad! How on earth did it happen?"

"Well, I've already told you about my doing my doctoral studies through an on-line university. The hours I had to spend in study were brutal – much worse than actually attending classes. My instructors were unsympathetic. So I worked exhausting hours to keep up. I was like a virtual zombie most of the time. Finally one day, right in the middle of my own lecture, I fell asleep on my feet."

"That's quite some trick! Did you fall? … Get hurt?"

"No – not physically. Thankfully, I was leaning against my desk and only drifted off momentarily. It was quite obvious, though, because my speech trailed off and I suddenly awakened with a snort."

"A snort? How did the class respond?"

"They were roaring with laughter … they thought it was hilarious and that started the nicknames and ridicule."

"Nicknames …? "

Phil proceeded to list many nicknames that his students gave him. "There were several - to mention a few, I was now 'Doc Snort', 'Doc Doze', and their favorite 'The Sleep Doctor – no mattress required'. I didn't have my degree yet but they knew I was working on it, so it was always Doc something."

"Well, if it's any consolation to you, I have a few doozeys myself."

"You?"

"Yes. But that's a topic for a later time. How long can you stay at your friend's place? Do you need to find someplace else? The entire lower level of my condo fully furnished. It's available rent free … if you're interested."

"Are you sure? – That's a very generous offer!"

"Absolutely! – I would really enjoy the company – it gets very lonely in my big place. When can you move in?"

"You need to know, Pete, this is a real answer to prayer!"

"Okay, Phil, we need to get something out in the air. We've been skirting around this whole religion matter for too long. Do you have something you want to say?"

"Yes, Pete, I am a believer." he said boldly.

"Well I guess we all believe in something – what's your take on religion?" Pete responded cautiously.

"When I say that I'm a believer, I mean I am a Bible believer – a Christian! What I'm saying, Pete, is that I'm a follower of Jesus Christ … born again … saved."

These were all familiar terms to Pete but he guarded his response saying: "Oh! I see – that's interesting. Growing up, I was very much involved in church. But lately – I've seemed to slip away. I guess you could say that I'm a backslider. To me, that's always been a rather descriptive word"

"What happened?"

"I think … hope … it's just a phase – but it's where I am right now. Maybe we can talk about my story next time we meet. My life has been shaken up and I've been seeking a solid foundation … something I can rely on."

"Yes, Pete, we need to talk … when you're ready."

The remaining few minutes before they ended their visit were spent discussing details about Phil's moving into Pete's condo – something that was exciting to both of them.

As Pete walked back home, he wondered if he had been too hasty in making his offer to Phil. *When I impulsively blurted it out it seemed like an excellent idea. Now, I will have to just go with the plan and hope for the best. We decided to make the move between Christmas and New Year's so I should know soon but the next few days should prove to be very interesting.*

He also thought about his comments about religion, wondering what impression this left on Phil. He seemed to have a very strong grip on his spiritual life. *Could this become an item of contention? What will he think of the life I'm living these days and issues that are tormenting me? Do I foresee problems?*

~

One day, just before last year's winter break, the esteemed Dr. P. T. Daniels moderated a panel discussion regarding the impact the existentialism of Kierkegaard, Nietzsche, Sartre, and Camus was making on modern culture and values. It was presented in one of the larger lecture halls on campus because attendance was required for all philosophy majors. With a crowd of several hundred, it was to be the highlight of their academic year. After introductory remarks and ground rules were laid for the discussion, they soon became involved in a truly spirited debate. Just as the discussion was reaching its most interesting point, a rather pompous senior stood and interrupted the panel.

"Dr. Daniels," he queried loudly "do you realize that you have acquired a substantial number of nicknames around campus lately? Does that cause you concern?"

Quite shocked – but not showing it, he replied: "Yes, Mr. Adams, I am quite aware of that fact. It doesn't bother me that much. But ... what does concern me is how you could consider that relevant to this event. However – do you have a favorite?"

Surprised and flustered by the prof's casual response, he replied rather sheepishly: "Well ... yes ... I do."

"Would you like to share it with the rest of us?" he asked calmly.

"Of the many, I prefer 'Dr. Maybe' because it most accurately sums up your inability to be responsible and show consideration to the university and its student body."

"Well then, why didn't you select 'Dr. No-show'?" he asked, demonstrating his knowledge of another option.

"With all due respect, you do show up for classes sometimes – we just never know when that will occur."

"Well, thanks for that much! I realize that my attendance record has been somewhat less than perfect. As I've been working my way through the grieving process, I know that I have let some of you down – that is about to change. By the way, how are things back home with 'The Addams Family'?" He immediately knew this question was in poor taste. It was rude and uncalled for and it missed its mark – Mr. Adams was considerably too young to have watched the ghoulish TV series several years ago. A few of the much older students snickered – mostly out of embarrassment for the professor and his obvious blunder.

He immediately apologized to Mr. Adams and tried to restore some semblance of order to the discussion.

"I'm truly sorry, Mr. Adams, for my unkind question. Although you didn't pick up on my sarcasm, I am indeed sorry and beg your forgiveness. This has been an curious interruption – however, we still have some time to get back to our previously scheduled topic."

Once everyone settled down, they resumed the rousing debate that was just underway before the nickname issue was brought to the forefront. Although stimulating, it didn't draw nearly as much attention or create the same excitement as the nickname discussion.

Various versions of this incident spread rapidly around the university campus. Within days the entire faculty and student body were aware that something rather unusual had taken place in that meeting. For many … details were rather vague but the results were very certain. It was an awkward time for everyone involved. Since this incident, Pete's attendance had improved considerably – but he still had some of the nicknames.

~

The details of the lab incident came back to Pete as he was trying to decide what he wanted to do about supper. *"Yes, Phil, I too, have nicknames."* His mind then drifted back to having a roommate.

Phil's living in the lower level of my place shouldn't present any problem. We can each have our own space and live our own lives ... I hope.

As he thought about Phil, the problem of his costly and embarrassing suspension troubled him. *What can I do to help ... beyond giving him a free place to live? We need to discuss this further. I can be a decent character witness. From our frequent interactions concerning maintenance details, I have come to know Phil – 'Jimmy' rather well. Can I become an amateur detective as well? Something is just too fishy about this robbery ... an expensive laptop computer and a new cell phone that was swiftly dumped in a hallway trash container.*

He decided to make a list of topics to discuss with Phil next time they meet.

Things to discuss with Phil

1. The move details

2. Housing arrangements

3. Financial matters

4. Restoring his job / reputation

5. Finding the real thief / motive

6.

He soon ran out of ideas but was certain, with more time and thought, his list would grow. *Soon we will begin my lengthy and somewhat tangled story. I'm not looking forward to it ... but, I guess, it needs to happen.*

~ Chapter Three ~

The bright December sun, peeking through the blinds in Pete's bedroom windows, gradually brought him to semi-consciousness. It was three days before Christmas. Phil had obtained permission from the authorities to leave the state, for a few days, to spend time with his mother and other family members back home in Indiana. This gave Pete the opportunity to spend time with his sons and their families. He had travelled to Georgia to see his daughter, son-in-law and two grandsons for Thanksgiving.

Time with his kids and their families was not the same since Julie died. It seemed that his primary role was, to bring grandma. He was most comfortable with older kids. This was true as long as he could remember – all the way back to the early days of their marriage. He coached the boys' softball and basketball teams and was able to persuade her to help sponsor the junior high youth group. She was best with the babies and younger ones, having served in the nursery and children's church.

Recently, since he had started dating, his sons asked that he not bring any of his lady friends with him. They said that their kids were not ready to see grandpa with some-one who was not their grandma. This limited the contact he had with his local grand kids. This Christmas he was invited to each of his son's houses … lone. Initially he had a problem with this conditional invitation – but he soon decided that it made sense.

Since he didn't have that many chances to be with his grandkids, he definitely planned to take advantage of this opportunity – even though it might be a bit awkward.

As he shaved, showered and prepared himself for the day, he reflected on how his life had changed in the past twenty-three months. *The joy and vigor are just not there. I once meditated on positive and encouraging things – now I am burdened down with doubts and heavy questions. Before Julie's death, I would often sing in the shower – now the song is gone.*

~

About five years ago, they had moved to Pleasant Meadows, a beautiful senior citizen's community, where they bought a very nice condo. They became involved in many neighborhood activities and rapidly made a number of new friends. After a couple years, Pete was elected as president of the village's association and took on the new responsibility with gusto. Julie was right there with him as a wonderful help and encouragement. Life was good!

During the early years in their new home, they noticed that some of the older residents were moving to assisted living homes – some were passing away. This prompted them to discuss their own mortality and what they should do as they reached that juncture in their lives. Pete first commented, "This will be a great place for you when I'm gone … with all the other widows and single ladies here. Of course, you would certainly be free to remarry – if you wanted to."

Her response caught him off guard "First, what makes you so sure you will go first? And second, I'm going to quote my mother on the idea of remarrying. When asked, after my father died, if she planned to marry again … she said 'What would I want with another old man?' You, on the other hand, would need another wife and you have my full blessing to get married again."

When he asked if she had any thoughts on how long he should wait she laughingly replied "At least wait until my body is cold in the grave." At that point the discussion moved to more end of life matters.

They talked about their desire to die together but never considered suicide. They knew life and death is not a thing they could control. So they gave up on the idea of going at the same time. Julie had been the main caregiver for her mom and both of Pete's parents, who all died slowly and painfully. She said that she would prefer not to experience that or be a burden to anyone. "You know, honey, if I could have my choice, I would prefer to die in my sleep." To Pete's total dismay that is exactly what happened a few years later.

About that same time, Julie asked Pete for a new set of golf clubs for her sixtieth birthday, which was coming up in February. He was quite surprised and asked why – since whenever they went out golfing she would just hit the ball a few times and then say "Give it a ride, honey." She told him that as they grew older this would give them something to do together ... since she knew he would not want to learn to sew.

Pete did just as she had asked. On Tuesdays, she would play in an all ladies league and he would play in a men's league. They would play together on Thursdays. Initially, she would score in the middle eighties for nine holes … taking the maximum of ten on most holes.

By the end of her first year, she was in the upper seventies and taking very few maximums. They were able to play most Tuesdays and Thursdays each season. By the end of the three seasons, Julie's game had improved steadily while Pete's seemed to get worse. One day, late in the fall, he shot a fifty and she had a fifty-nine. To make matters worse, he had a really bad round two days earlier – in his league … same course … same nine and had a sixty-one. This got his attention … he was once a high thirties and low forties golfer. Only half joking, he said "If your game keeps getting better and mine keeps getting worse – I may just have to take up sewing."

They had no idea that would be one of their last times to play golf together. She died suddenly from a massive heart attack the following January. He was so thankful for the times that they had spent together – both on the golf course and on his book signing tours. Although he now missed her dearly, they had enjoyed forty-four years together. That was an amazing blessing and bonus, since he almost lost her giving birth to their first son, only eighteen months after their wedding.

~

When his mind came back to the present, he continued to prepare himself for the visit with Stan and his family. So many times, since Julie's death, he had mentally replayed everything from their exhilarating family events to their calm, intimate talks. But today, he needed to focus on his granddaughters. He had to control his grief in front of them. They were dealing with the loss of both grandmas in the last four years. Now, at the ages of ten and eight, it was a very big time of adjustment. He needed to be strong for his family. This was no easy task – especially on family holidays. He recalled his visit last Christmas.

The girls seemed to act as though nothing had changed in their young lives. Were they just in denial or had they learned from their other grandma's death that life goes on and they must too? They had been just as playful and giddy as usual ... happy and bubbly - bundles of energy and Christmas joy.

When he arrived at Stan and Sophia's home their girls raced to the door to greet him and nearly bowled him over with their enthusiastic hugs. The mouthwatering aroma of the traditional prime rib dinner filled the whole house and wafted out the front door to welcome him.

He removed his shoes – an old family custom – went to the beautiful living room and settled into an overstuffed couch. The Stanley Daniels family had attained quite a luxurious lifestyle, thanks to the success of the Daniels and Daniels Law Firm. Their elegant home was just one example of that success.

After what seemed like forever, everyone was called to the table – where they stood behind their chairs for the prayer. Once they had prayed, Pete just stood behind his chair admiring the culinary presentation. It was breath-taking!

The first couple years of their marriage, Stan did most of the cooking ... he worked as a cook during his college days. Sophia soon became an excellent cook, after she became hooked on Martha Stewart and a several other famous food prep experts.

Now she and Stan were a phenomenal duo in the kitchen. The holiday feasts they put on were fit for a king! Pete always looked forward to this meal. He often said "It's a spread that will make me spread – maybe so much that I won't not fit through their door to go home." This was certainly an overstatement – but they all seemed to enjoy it just the same … especially the girls as they visualized it and giggled profusely. Of course, they had to add their own comments on the subject.

As they were enjoying the feast, Stan asked him how things were going at the university.

He replied, "The freshman class enrollment is up twenty percent this year and campus enthusiasm is at an all-time high. However, the high spirits aren't being experienced by everyone."

"How so, dad?" Stan asked seeming a bit puzzled.

"We had a theft in my building recently. A fancy laptop and new cell phone were stolen from a prof's office. My friend is on an unpaid suspension – as a suspect."

"Do you think he did it?"

"Definitely not! He is a man of high moral character."

"What is he doing to exonerate himself … Does he have any legal counsel ... Is anyone helping him?"

"I invited him to move into the lower level of my condo until he can get back on his feet financially. His reserve funds are rapidly diminishing. His family is poor and living in another state. His situation is desperate – to say the least! He certainly can't afford an attorney."

Leaning forward, Stan asked "Is he one of your colleagues? Do you think he would accept any outside help?"

Warming to his son's obvious interest, Pete responded "He's the head custodian in my building and I think he would gladly accept any help he could get. What do you have in mind?"

"Well, David and I have been very busy and making money hand over fist so to speak and are looking for a couple worthy pro bono cases to show our appreciation. Know what I mean? We want to help someone who really needs it."

"Well ... I ..."

"Could we do some investigating and offer some legal assistance? Would this help?" He seemed quite excited.

"I'm sure it would. Should I mention it to David when I'm at their place?" Pete was excited too.

Stan encouraged him to bring it up so David would be prepared for a future discussion. They agreed to meet and determine their strategy in the next few days.

When they had finished dinner, they moved to the family room to exchange gifts. After several hours of fun, games and laughter, Pete excused himself and left for home.

It was great to be with family! What do people do when they don't have family support?

Driving home, he was in much better spirits. He was thankful for his family …

They have all turned out so well. I'm certain Julie would be proud of them as well. Parenting hadn't always been easy –

but it was worth the effort ... every bit of it! Now I'm seeing the next generation, the grandchildren, growing into bright and beautiful young people. When we were all playing table games, both Joy and Gracie were right in there ... competing with the adults. They had certainly inherited the Daniels' desire to win.

Happy and exhausted, he went to bed soon after arriving home. Sound sleep overtook him in short order and he had a wonderfully restful night.

~ Chapter Four ~

December twenty-third ... two days before Christmas ... home alone ... very alone. Here I am alone in my thoughts again. Is this going to be one of those difficult days the grief counselors caution about? I was so strong in those early days ... even encouraging those who tried to encourage me. What is happening to me now?

~

January nineteenth of 2009 will always be a day deeply etched in Pete's mind. That morning, he and Julie planned to go to his office to prepare for a conference they regularly attended in Washington D. C. He was to speak and sign his books at a prestigious annual event. She typically got up an hour before him and prepared herself for the day. A pot of hot coffee was always a part of this routine. When Pete got up, he saw her sitting in her recliner. He could tell she was not feeling well because she was still in her robe. When he asked what was wrong, she replied that she was experiencing flu like symptoms – not surprisingly since almost everyone they knew seemed to be battling it … and losing. Pete decided to stay home with Julie and tend to her needs.

Right after a light lunch, Julie suggested that Pete go to the office and take care of his preparation for the trip. He agreed but promised to be home by four o'clock. When he walked in the door, he was surprised to see her fully dressed, hair brushed, makeup on and smiling brightly.

He said "You look great. How do you feel?"

She replied "I feel much better now. I guess I just had that twenty-four hour flu bug that's going around."

They chatted and discussed their plans for the pending trip and the time they were to spend in Florida right after the convention. They had reservations for the entire month of February … away from the bitter cold and heavy snowfalls common to Michigan.

After a light supper, they watched the news, Wheel of Fortune and Jeopardy – standard viewing for seniors. About eight-fifteen, Julie excused herself and went to the bathroom. Coming out, she said "If I keep that up, I'm going to lose weight."

When Pete asked her what happened, she told him that she had vomited up everything that she had eaten that day. He then asked her how she felt and if she was weak.

Her surprising reply was "I feel great!"

With that reassurance, Pete went to his office in the front of the house and Julie went to bed. That was just after eight-thirty.

About thirty minutes later, Pete went back to their bedroom to check on Julie again. The moonlight, coming through the blinds, offered just enough light for Pete to tell she was not in bed. He traced his way back through the house … hot tub room … bathroom … everywhere.

When he went back into the bedroom, he looked on the other side of the bed and found her. She had fallen out of bed and was lying on the floor between the bed and the wall. She had done that once before and slept right through the whole thing. Pete thought she had done it again. When he attempted to awaken her, there was no response. Immediately, he called 911 and they dispatched emergency vehicles to their home.

As they were on their way the operator talked Pete through CPR in an attempt to revive her. The paramedics arrived within just a few minutes and quickly started their expert procedures. After about thirty minutes of strenuous effort they pronounced Julie dead at ten o'clock. Once the coroner had removed her body, about 11:30, Pete called their daughter in Georgia and their two sons. The boys both came to be with him and stayed until they were satisfied that he was okay. During this time they reflected on Julie's favorite Bible verses and looked through several hymnals to find her special hymns. This was also a precious time of comfort to them. They left at about three a.m.

The next morning Pete called his pastor and Don, his best friend in the community and frequent golfing partner. They came and spent several hours with him. Friends, especially Christian friends, were a true encouragement to Pete. During the time they were there, a steady flow of well-wishers stopped by the Daniels' home while dozens more called him on the phone. His pastor was quite amused at the number of times Pete was the one giving hope and encouragement to his guests. He knew very well that his God was in control and his beloved was now rejoicing in Glory.

He was sad for his loss but took comfort in knowing that his Lord was too wise to make mistakes and too loving to be cruel. Some older folk, including a very aged aunt, said "It's just not right. She was so young. I should have gone first." Pete reminded them that we should never question the wisdom or goodness of God. "He is God … we are not!"

The visitation for friends and family was held on January twenty-third – Pete's sixty-eighth birthday. Hundreds of friends and relatives came out to show respect for Julie and to extend their sympathy to Pete. He and his immediate family were amazed at the overwhelming show of support.

Hundreds attended Julie's funeral service, including a full busload and several cars from Pleasant Meadows. Pete and each of their three grown kids read tributes to Julie and appeared to be experiencing that "Amazing Grace" people often refer to quite glibly. When one lady said "You are just in denial. Someday you will come to your senses and know what hit you." His reply was that he had seen his wife dead and tried to revive her. He knew she was gone – but to a far better place. In a strange way, he sensed that he had met one of 'Job's comforters.' He quietly reminded himself that a person needed to be wise and careful when trying to comfort the grieving. Good intentions needed to be coupled with kind and gentle words.

The funeral service was a celebration of Julie's life. She had been a good child and an 'all A' student throughout her entire time in school – graduating as valedictorian of her high school class and at the top of her nursing school class. One Sunday night, her date took her to his church where she heard the gospel for the first time. That night, she learned that she was a sinner and not worthy of God's perfect heaven. She knelt beside her bed and asked

Jesus to forgive her and come into her heart. From that day until her death Julie was a new person – not just a good person but a child of God.

Her life was filled with joy, comfort and purpose. Her exemplary life, and several verses she had underlined in her Bible, gave the pastor plenty of material for his brief sermon. The congregation sang her favorite songs and hymns in between the pastor's comments. Her all-time favorite, one she often played on the piano, was It is Well With My Soul. She especially liked verses two and three:

"My sin, oh the joy of this glorious thought,
My sin, not in part, but the whole,
Is nailed to the cross, and I bear it no more.
Praise the Lord, Praise the Lord, O my soul!

And, Lord haste the day when my faith shall be sight,
The clouds be rolled back as a scroll:
The trump shall resound and the Lord shall descend,
Even so, it is well with my soul!

It is well, with my soul,
It is well; it is well with my soul!"

The words of the third verse refer to what many scholars call the Rapture. In answer to Julie's prayers and strong commitment to her Lord Jesus Christ, she didn't have to wait for that day. "Absent from the body present with the Lord." Everyone commented on the beautiful service.

~

Every time Pete thought about losing his Julie, he was initially sad. But, as he thought through the entire time and process, he was able to rejoice for their forty-four wonderful years together.

They had enjoyed many great memories as a family. He knew she wouldn't want to see him this sad, wallowing in grief and self-pity. *So, Pete, What are you going to do today to make a difference in someone else's life? I can almost hear Julie saying "That's more like it, mister!"*

Now he was in a positive frame of mind and started to make plans for the day he would be spending with his son, David, and his family. David and Marie have four very active kids – three girls and finally a son. Nathan. They are expecting number five, gender unknown, next April.

He planned to mention, briefly, his conversation with Stan about Phil's plight and the possibility of their firm coming to his aid. This would lay some groundwork for their meeting next week. They would not be able to go into any detail because the house would be filled from floor to ceiling throughout … with 'happy boisterosity'! He knew that wasn't a word – but it was the best way to describe it.

All eight of his grandkids are extremely active and very intelligent. Their parents have dedicated a great deal of attention to teaching them – even before they were school age.

His children are definitely a heritage from the Lord – his grandchildren make it that much better. They bring him great joy and keep him young … if he could just keep up with them.

As he thought about tomorrow, his heart warmed. It promised to be another wonderful day filled with excitement and joy!

~ Chapter Five ~

Christmas Eve day arrived and it was another cold and blustery Michigan day. Pete would spend today with his other son David and his family. In earlier years, Pete and Julie would have their three children and spouses over for a feast on Christmas day. As the families grew, their children decided it worked out best to have their parents spend a day around Christmas in each of their homes. This allowed the young families to spend Christmas day on their own. It was a bit awkward scheduling time with each family and not interfering with their time alone and with their in-laws – but it was worth it.

Once Pete had completed the ritual of getting ready for the day, he ate a small breakfast and started rounding up all the gifts for the grandkids. Julie had been much better at selecting appropriate items for the little ones – but he tried.

He wondered how many people would be there today. David's family usually celebrated special days with a full house – literally! They had in-laws, friends, clients and more in-laws … all with their offspring – of course.

What a crowd – it's a 'happy boisterosity!' There's no way to conceal a David Daniels shindig. Cars fill their private parking lot, overflow into their circular driveway and spill out onto the private drive leading to their home. Daniels and Daniels' success affords David's family the opportunity to enjoy some of the finer things in life – and share them.

The drive to David's home was much more enjoyable in the summer when Pete could have the top down in his sporty convertible. But he was thankful that, in spite of the frigid temperatures, the roads were clear and dry. His trip across town and into the swanky suburbs was a pleasant one. He was able to relax to the sounds of his favorite instrumental CD's featuring many great hymns and gospel songs.

He even surprised himself by singing along with the more familiar ones. Although not a great singer, he could carry a tune – on his better days. He had often told Julie that his voice was best suited for singing in the shower. But … today he was singing! There was something very therapeutic about that – and he knew it. The thought of being with his family again was refreshing and invigorating. He was keenly aware of how exhausting the large and exuberant crowd could be, but he was prepared and considered it a happy exchange.

Time seemed to speed by, thanks to the music, and he almost drove by the entrance to David's gated upscale community. As he made his way down the winding tree-lined main drive, he came to Daniels' Courtyard. It was the name David's family had selected for their private drive. Pete affectionately referred to it as 'Lawyer's Lane.'

As he had expected, the whole area looked like a parking lot for a ritzy yacht club. *So, here we go ... another big David Daniels' celebration!*

In honor of the Christmas holiday, the Daniels' house staff was given the week off – so the children were the official greeters and the women of the family all pitched in and prepared the meals.

Pete was enthusiastically welcomed by all his grandkids in one huge 'group hug.' Once inside, he handed his coat to the oldest and initiated a conversation with her – only to be interrupted by the others, who all had their exciting stories to tell.

After spending several minutes with his grandkids, Pete worked his way into the areas where the adults were conversing. They were just as excited as the youngsters. There was a literal buffet of discussions going on in most of the rooms on the main level of the enormous house. In the dining hall several ladies were discussing the latest 'news' from their neighborhoods and their various social clubs. In the vast kitchen other ladies … of a less affluent sort were sharing favorite recipes and doting on their 'brighter-than-average' offspring. In the library, several men were attempting to 'one-up' each other with their latest business deals or investment coups.

Another group of men, mostly husbands of the ladies in the kitchen, had found their way to the recreation room. Appropriately, they were discussing their favorite college and professional football teams – and, of course, who would win the Super Bowl. A few of David's closer friends had discovered his 'man cave' and were admiring his many trophies. Meanwhile, David's father-in-law, a suave CEO of his own public relations firm, moved from discussion to discussion … sharing his wisdom with any and all willing listeners.

Pete soon caught David's attention and was immediately introduced to several of his new friends and clients. Pete got the impression that many of the more successful guests were surprised to meet a professor who had some appreciable taste in his wardrobe.

He silently guessed they had seen too many movies like 'The Absent-minded Professor' and had formed their own stereotypes of how a Doctor of Philosophy should look. He thoroughly enjoyed meeting each of them and secretly analyzing them. He, too, could play the mind games – but not wanting to offend – he kept it all to himself. He sensed a healthy spiritual atmosphere throughout the home. Some of it seemed a bit pharisaical, as with many such gatherings, but it was mostly genuine and refreshing.

Having been duly introduced to the men's groups, Pete found Marie in the kitchen and asked where he should put the gifts for the grandkids. She said he could just bring them to the kitchen and she would hide them until tomorrow. Outside, he decided that the cold fresh air was a nice change from the crowd warmth in the house. Though there were many children noisily playing, the openness of the outdoors made the noise more tolerable. All of this 'happy boisterosity' was a huge change from the 'solemn tranquility' he experienced alone in his condo.

He did hope having Phil living in his lower level rooms would bring a bit more life to his place. Briefly, his mind went to Phil's plight and he remembered that, somehow, he needed to talk to David about helping with his legal issue.

After bringing the gifts to the kitchen, he heard David call everyone to the dining room where the feast was ready for all to enjoy. Marie, her mom and sisters had prepared the meal – enough food to feed an army.

With the crowd finally assembled, David led everyone in a beautiful prayer of thanks and praise to the Lord for His bountiful provisions. For a few moments, as they all were passing platters and filling their plates, the only sounds were the clinking of forks and serving spoons on fine China. Once all the platters had been passed, almost like clockwork, the conversations resumed. Subject matters were diverse and voices seemed to echo throughout the room. Pete decided that trying to follow any one conversation was futile – so he sat quietly eating the wonderful home cooked meal and enjoyed the bedlam.

Once the feast had satisfied everyone – and perhaps over satisfied some, the guests started to excuse themselves while the family remained to clean up and relax from a busy day. This, finally, gave Pete the opportunity to talk briefly with David about helping Phil.

Pete gave David the basics of Phil's case and mentioned that he had also discussed it with Stan. David agreed to meet with them after the holidays ... once he and Stan were back in their office. He seemed pleased that his dad was interested in having them come to the aid of a friend. Pete knew that he could not find anyone more competent to work on Phil's behalf – and all free. He thanked David and his family, giving everyone a loving hug, and headed home.

The December days were short in Michigan so his drive home, in the darkness, was more challenging than his trip over in the daylight. But he was awake, alive and in a great frame of mind – it went very well.

Arriving at his condo, he was pleased at the thought of his two sons. W*orking together for all of their adult lives and ... so successfully! Growing up they were best of friends* *or fiercest enemies. They were only nineteen months apart in age and were extremely competitive. People have said that was a trait they inherited from me. How could that be – I had no siblings?*

His sons had carried on the family name with diligence and dignity. It was not always easy for them and they each had to learn to make some important spiritual choices based upon their own commitment to Christ. They learned rather early that a second hand faith was no faith at all. Now, as fathers, they were instilling the same values and faith practices in their children. To Pete, this was a reward far greater than he could have ever dreamt. It couldn't have come at a better time because he needed this kind of affirmation. *Yes! My parents' faith, Julie's faith and my faith ... what's left of it ... that faith is still working today.* He knew it in his heart … why did he have such doubts in his head?

As he entered his dimly lit condo, he seemed to sense his answer … he was alone. How could a place that was so full of life when Julie was there become such a drab habitation with her gone? Pete's life had become one big emotional roller coaster. He had his highs, which kept him going, and his lows that made him wonder if it was worth the struggle. Tonight, however, he was concentrating on the joys of the day. After watching some of the news – another downer – he drifted off to sleep in his recliner. He was suddenly awakened by an obnoxiously loud commercial by one of the local car dealerships. Wearily he trudged off to bed. He didn't set an alarm … he knew tomorrow was Christmas day and he had no plans.

~ Chapter Six ~

Christmas morning, a Sunday, rolled around just like any other day for Pete. Attending church alone was not in his plans. He had already celebrated with his family and Phil was still away for two more days. How different life was since Julie's death. Two years ago they had taken the trip south to spend Christmas with their daughter and her family. That was their last Christmas together – she died just three weeks after their return. He had read in a book a friend had given him, that weekends, special family times and holidays were the loneliest for people dealing with grief. How true that was – and he had a double dose because December 26 would have been their forty-sixth wedding anniversary.

Pete trudged out to his porch to get the morning Press. No paper? After searching a bit, he found it wedged in the shrubs – somewhat ragged and wet from the snow.

Is it going to be one of those days? I hope my nosy neighbor isn't watching me climb through the bushes in my boxer shorts, robe and slippers. She would be quite amused by the crazy antics of a sophisticated professor in one of his less dignified moments. I will, without a doubt, hear about it if she did. She'll spread it throughout the local grapevine. Who knows, she might even put it in the local news.

Back in his warm condo, he brewed some coffee and made brunch – it was too late to be breakfast. Unshaven, disheveled and half awake, Pete started his way into what should be a Merry Christmas.

How times had changed. The silence is deafening.

As he peeled apart the half-soaked paper on his kitchen table, he set aside all the after Christmas sale ads … clearly half of the Christmas day edition. He remembered when the newspaper was just that – mostly news, some small ads and a few full pages of department store ads. Now there were numerous full color glossy tabloids promoting everything from ladies apparel to camping and sports gear. He gave a sympathetic sigh … *I feel sorry for the poor little guy who has to deliver these monsters.* But, he was happy to have this soggy, tattered friend with which to spend part of his lonely day. *Billy ... Willy? He's a good kid – but he needs to work on his throwing arm. I hope he has a nice Christmas with his family – if he has one.*

Having arranged the sections in the order in which he usually read them, he was preparing to read the national news, but his eye was distracted by the local news. There was a new section he hadn't noticed before. It featured several local families who were experiencing hard times … loss of employment, apartment fires, serious medical issues and a whole range of heartaches that called for caring individuals to "come alongside and show some special love." *That sounds a lot like a financial commitment I could make. I've never been involved with something like this – except for my new venture with Phil. Ah yes ... Phil could help. It would be good for both of us. How soon could we start?*

Pete read several of the articles and decided to set that section aside for further discussion with Phil. *I wonder if my students might enjoy supporting this project.*

"Whoa, boy!" he said aloud "Let's take it a step at a time."

Before he finished the local news section, he quickly scanned the obituaries – a habit he started about the time his father died about twenty years ago. He knew that seemed rather morbid to his family but it helped him keep up with developments in his friends' lives. The trend seemed to move seamlessly from the deaths of his friends' parents to the final departure of his friends – even to the death of his own wife. Having experienced the loss of both parents and his wife, he was able to be more sensitive to the deep heartaches the survivors were feeling. Although his goal was to comfort and encourage them, he was always relieved to not find anyone he knew listed.

Another feature in the local section, a happier one, was the colorful pages of engagement, wedding and anniversary announcements. Pete started reading these shortly after graduating from high school. He watched as many of his classmates married – most before him and a few after. Then, he was out of town continuing his education, starting his family and busy with all the activities of life and he lost track of many of his friends.

When he finally moved back to the Grand Rapids area, he was back to reading these pages again. There were the same features he remembered from several years ago. He soon was able to find friends' anniversaries and, now, their children's wedding announcements. Today, as he read the anniversary announcements, his heart was heavy. Tomorrow would be their forty-sixth anniversary. But now … he was alone … very alone. He hadn't been content to be alone. A couple weeks after Julie's death he read in Genesis 2:18:

> "The Lord God said, "It is not good for man to be alone. I will make a helper suitable for him."

He had read that verse numerous times, but it never struck him as directly as it did then. In the last twenty-three months, Pete had been vigilant in trying to find that special person that God had prepared for him.

Pete finished reading the paper and decided to take a nap. Sleeping helped him pass the time and was something he was more inclined to do during some of his lonely times. He read in one of his books on grieving that sorrowing individuals require more sleep. It worked for him.

He was awakened to the sound of carolers at his front door. As he peered out the window, no one was there. He had, apparently had a dream about her – the blond! She did come caroling at this time last year. When he opened the door back then, he choked out a tearful "Thanks and Merry Christmas to you too." *What was she trying to do to my fragile emotions? Oh well, that's over ... or is it? Now she's still in my dreams.*

He spent some time thinking about her and rehashing his 'roller coaster' dating days of last year. His thoughts went back to a few months after Julie's death.

I removed my wedding ring and started to notice the ladies as I would grocery shop. I tried, as coyly as possible, to notice if they were wearing a wedding ring. I also had a new interest in attractive ladies who were eating alone in my favorite restaurants. I usually ate out because it was a pain to cook for one. I wasn't ready to start dating per se. Becoming more observant of the prospects was nerve wracking enough. I learned quickly that there were many self-appointed cupids and matchmakers – who were more than willing to help. My standard reply was "I'll be fine, please let me do this my way." I had no idea how many twists and turns would develop in 'my way.'

One thing Pete soon realized was that dating as a mature adult – a senior citizen – was totally different than dating as a teen. Not only was he very set in his ways … so were the ladies. Life's experiences – some good … some bad – all have an effect on relationships. His friends called it "The Baggage Factor." It also seemed as though many of the 'rules' had changed. It was a whole new ball game. As a veteran at the old dating game, he was a rookie now.

Thanks to computers and the internet, there were several new tools that had been invented since his youth. With these tools, came a whole new search strategy and a strange language called 'computereze.' A few days after Julie's death, his son, David, set him up on Facebook. He called it 'a social media', where Pete could meet people 'online' and 'friend' them. This new discovery became a real comfort to him. It gave him a way to reconnect with his friends - some from many years ago. Mostly, it kept him occupied. It gave him something to do on those long and lonely winter days. Interestingly, it was there that he made contacts that resulted in his first several dates.

Before he actually started dating, he met with various lady friends for lunch – not as 'dates' but as friendly chats and fun times together. From these casual meetings, he soon learned that many women had experienced some very devastating lives in their previous marriages. He listened to sad stories of abuse, infidelity and just plain meanness ... such a contrast to his life with Julie. Every gal he talked to seemed to have similar tales of woe. This upset him greatly and he wondered ...

What are my chances of finding that special person? Chance? My life isn't determined by chance. That's just crazy!

One day, while on Facebook, Pete was surprised to find a girl he dated a couple times while in college. After many 'messages' and 'chats' they agreed to meet and spend a couple days getting reacquainted. She lived on the other side of the state, so he stayed in a motel a few miles from her place. Although they had a nice time - there was no spark … no romantic interest. On his way home, he had some time to brood on his dilemma. When he got home, he sent her a message stating that he felt it was too soon after Julie's death to start a serious relationship. "Let's just continue our friendship for now" he wrote. This all happened at the end of May – just over four months after losing Julie.

In early June, Pete discovered on Facebook an attractive blond also from his almamater. She looked familiar, but he knew they were not there at the same time – so he asked her to 'friend' him. She agreed even though she wasn't sure they actually knew each other. After several Facebook conversations and a couple phone calls, they agreed to meet. She was going to the city's big annual festival with a singles group from her church. Pete had planned to attend as well – alone. They decided to meet at eight o'clock at a certain venue.

Pete went early and enjoyed some of the ethnic delights he could only find at the festival food tents. As he walked up and down the several streets of celebration, he became painfully aware of the concept 'alone in a crowd.' He saw families, groups of teens and couples holding hands enjoying each other's company. He was alone ... no friends ... no family ... no one to hold his hand ... alone! With more than thirty different groups selling dishes from all around the world, he chose two different meat dishes and a chocolate ice cream cone. It was a hot sunny day and some of the chocolate dripped onto his shirt.

Oh, great! It would have to be right on a big white stripe where it's so obvious. Now what can I do?

When the city clock struck eight, Pete was at the tent where they decided to meet – ice cream stain and all. He spotted the attractive little blond and awkwardly moved toward her.

"Excuse me, miss" he asked "Can you tell me how to get a chocolate stain out of my shirt?"

She promptly replied "If you can you tell me how to get an orange chalk stain out of mine?" She had accidently brushed against some graffiti.

After a good laugh, the ice was broken in a way neither of them anticipated. This was the beginning of a special friendship – that grew into a fond relationship – and they dated weekly for nearly four months. Although they didn't realize it at first, they soon discovered their paths had crossed several times over the years. Their children even knew each other. It seemed like destiny!

On one of their early dates they encountered a couple who knew their families. They both had the same reaction … "We better tell our kids before they hear it second hand." Since she had been divorced for a number of years – and her ex had remarried – her sons were happy for their mom. Pete's family appeared to be fine with the situation as well. After their breakup, he learned his sons just weren't ready to see their dad dating that soon. He seriously wondered *will they ever be.* He certainly was. His daughter was supportive at every turn – and there were several turns on Pete's road to recovery.

They enjoyed the entire summer attending concerts at various parks and campgrounds, church picnics and some special times with friends. She was a fine Christian lady with very high principles and a lot of fun!

Pete had strong feelings for her and he couldn't deny it. Each time he told her how much he cared for her; she seemed ill at ease and said she sensed he was without thinking transferring his love for Julie to her. When she didn't give Pete the answers he longed for, he would back off and suggest they stop seeing each other. To this she would reply "Are you bailing on me?" It seems this conversation would come up every three to four weeks.

When he asked what type of guy she was looking for she answered "Just like you … like Jesus." Shocked, he knew it was impossible to live up to her expectations – and he told her just that. She just laughed and said "Don't put yourself down."

Pete was certainly still hurting from the loss of his Julie but he sincerely believed that they were meant to be a couple – for the rest of their lives. Each time he coaxed her for some kind of commitment, their ties seemed to weaken.

Those tense times finally led to their parting ways in late September – not on the friendliest terms. In retrospect, Pete suspected he was in too much of a hurry to find a new companion. *Would it have worked if we had met at a later time ... well ... maybe? There still would have been some major hurdles – and hurdling wasn't my track event. I was a dash man. That's it! I was in too much of a rush. Have I learned my lesson? Maybe ...*

After four months seeing the same lady, Pete decided to be more casual in his dating. He needed some time to recover from his first serious relationship since losing Julie. This helped.

As part of this new approach, he signed up with a couple different internet Christian dating sites and began to study the many profiles of available ladies in his area. Once he had eliminated most of them, he contacted the one he found most alluring and they met for pizza at one of his favorite eateries. The hostess seated them next to a table occupied by some very noisy and rude characters. Conversation was difficult – but the food was great. As they walked to her car, he apologized and asked if he could see her again in a few days ... someplace where they could talk and hear each other. She said "No thanks, I don't think I'm interested." It caught Pete off guard.

It's not supposed to work that way. I'm usually the one who decided not to ask for a second date.

On the way back to his car he said to himself "Oh well, there are plenty of other fish in the pond."

Recently, he had heard about a friend who attended a singles activity at a local church where he saw this very attractive lady. This guy, being very timid, nervously asked if he could sit next to her. She laughed in his face and loudly spurted "I'm already with someone, little man." He was so humiliated that he never went back to that group. He gave up any hope of finding a companion. He's still living alone.

Unlike his friend, Pete determined ... *I will not quit – that's just not my style.*

~ Chapter Seven ~

Pete was relieved to have survived Christmas day and today was his anniversary. He would be making final preparations for Phil's arrival. He was totally ready for the holidays to be over and looking forward to helping Phil move in. They hoped to get him settled in before classes started for the new calendar year. Phil would arrive home later today and Pete was to meet him at the bus station.

The next few days promised to be busy … but, definitely therapeutic. It doesn't take a special degree to know that helping others is one of the best ways to help oneself. He was certainly anticipating having some good one-on-one conversations with his new friend and confidant. He couldn't wait to tell Phil that his sons were willing and eager to take on his case … free! Phil's bus wasn't due until five o'clock, so he had plenty of time to anticipate their meeting. After a light brunch, Pete spent a few hours doing various errands, tidying up his condo and planning for Phil's big arrival.

When the big old Greyhound pulled into the station, it belched out the usual nauseating diesel fumes. Pete didn't even notice. His mind was focused upon seeing his friend and sharing their holiday experiences. When Phil stepped down from the bus, Pete barely recognized him. Phil was sporting a neatly trimmed mustache and goatee. He had a very stylish haircut and was wearing all new clothes. He was the very image of the dignified Psyc professor that he aspired to be.

He was a new man! It was obvious that he was in good spirits and had experienced a great visit with his family. He also appeared to be happy to be back on his new home turf. They were like brothers reuniting after a long absence – in a way they were.

Once Pete had recovered from seeing 'the new Phil', he shouted out "Hey, Doc, are you ready for supper?"

Without hesitation Phil replied, "Yes I am!"

As they walked to the car Pete couldn't contain himself. "What happened to you? You look great … you win the lottery or something?" He knew Phil wasn't a gambler but he was at a loss for words.

Phil chuckled "No, but I had an amazing visit and can't wait to tell you about it. Where are we eating?"

They decided the downtown Big Boy would be a good change of pace. It was close to the bus station and right by the Grand Rapids GVSU campus. They weren't in the habit of eating at student hangouts, but were both hungry and it was convenient – so that settled it.

After their waitress had taken their order, Pete spoke right up "Okay! Let's hear it … the whole story!"

"Well" he started "you recall I haven't seen my family in several years now. Things have changed on the old home front. Mom is doing well … aging – but doing well. My younger sisters are both married with families. The two youngest brothers, who were teens when I was last there, have completed four years of college … on scholarships. My next younger brothers have become successful in the hardware business. They are the ones responsible for my new look. Pretty snazzy, don't you think?"

Pete just chuckled and nodded his approval. "So you had a satisfying visit then? That's great!"

"As I said before, it was amazing – far better than I ever expected! Now the ride there and back was not that great but my stay could not have been better. My brothers wanted to pay for a plane ticket back. Since I already had my return bus ticket, I didn't want them to waste their money. They seem to have all they need – but I believe in living frugally."

Pete asked if he had mentioned his situation with his family and, if so, how they responded. He indicated that he did and that they were very supportive.

When their food came there was a period of silence and Phil prayed silently. When he finished, Pete indicated that it would be fine if he prayed aloud for both of them next time. This brought a big smile to Phil's face.

As they enjoyed their supper, the conversation shifted to their food, the youthful clientele and small talk. As they surveyed the other diners, Phil noticed a homeless man cowering in a corner booth. He appeared to have just come in from the cold and was trying awkwardly not to be conspicuous – but he stood out like a sore thumb … a very sore thumb! This fellow's plight must have touched Phil. He asked our waitress to take his order and bring him the bill. She agreed and seemed impressed at his generosity. Phil, softly - gently, said something about

"As you do it to the least of these …"

The words rang clearly in Pete's mind. He realized that this was truly a spiritual moment. Phil paid the homeless man's bill and gave the young waitress a generous tip. She thanked him in tears and said "God bless you, sir!"

"Yes, ma'am, He does far more than I deserve."

The two men stayed there for some time, ordered dessert and returned to their discussion about Phil's trip. Pete was obviously distracted momentarily by his friend's quiet and humble act of kindness. Phil broke the silence, slightly startling Pete, who was deep in thought. "My brothers, the ones in the hardware business, want me to move back there and run one of their stores for them."

Caught totally off guard, Pete said "What … you run a hardware store? Nuts, bolts and things like that … think you'd enjoy that?"

Phil laughed "It's a job. The pay would be good. . I told them I would think – and pray about it. Of course, I need to solve my problems at Grand Valley first."

"I want to discuss that with you, Phil, but we need to talk about this matter right now. What about your plans … degrees … career goals?"

"Well, I …"

Before he could continue, Pete interrupted "You're the Psyc major, Phil, but it seems to me like you're selling yourself short."

"Remember, Pete, I've been working as a janitor – so this would be a step up."

"Okay, I guess you have a point there. Now let's shift gears here. Have you heard anything more about your suspension and the investigation?"

"No! The state police have taken over and I haven't heard anything from them. Campus security people know me and are sympathetic – but it's out of their hands. Now it's become a big fiasco!"

"Well, Phil, when I told my sons about your dilema they both, immediately, said they want to help you pro bono! That is if you are comfortable with their involvement. They are among the best in their field."

"I know. I've seen them on TV handling some very high profile cases. Do they think mine is that major?"

Pete chuckled. "No, but I sense they would enjoy a change of pace. That's not to imply that they would treat your case lightly or give you any less than their best."

"If they are anything like their father, I'm sure they will do a great job. Yes, I would be most grateful for any help they are willing to give. You did say this was pro bono ... no charge ... right?"

"That's the way they want it. If you don't mind, I'd like to sit in on your conversations with them. It would be interesting to see them in operation. All I know now is that David oversees most of the investigation work; and Stan's staff handles the trials and legal matters."

"Sounds good to me! I'm excited that they want to help!"

"Fine, I'll get back to my sons regarding a meeting time that will fit their schedule. I'm guessing we can meet any time in the next week or so."

"I certainly can!"
"In the meantime, you may want to be thinking of ... gathering up information that will expedite your case."

"Wow, Doc, it sounds like you could handle my case!"

"Let's leave it to the professionals. We should go now."

As they were leaving, the homeless man waved and gave them a toothless smile.

Once in Pete's sporty new car, they headed for Phil's temporary residence. As soon as the heater was blowing warm air, Phil breathed in deeply and commented about the new car aroma.

Pete responded almost apologetically "Yeah, my old one was starting to be too costly in repairs ... so I splurged and got this new toy."

"Nice car, Pete, It isn't bad to have nice things as long as they don't become idols ... just watch your priorities."

Satisfied that he would not be branded a selfish hedonist, Pete asked "Okay, now how do we get to your place?"

Having the directions clear in his mind, he continued to lead the conversation. "Can we start to move your things into my place tomorrow?"

They agreed to Pete's picking him up at nine and having breakfast at McDonalds. While there, they could start making plans.

Driving home, Pete thought *well, tomorrow is the big day! I certainly hope this all works out and I'm not making a big mistake. I guess I'll know soon.*

As he approached his condo, he pressed the button to his garage door opener. *Handy little luxury on a cold winter night. I like being spoiled ... is that wrong? Poor Phil he has missed so much ... or has he?*

It was late. He crawled into his nice warm bed and was asleep in minutes.

~ Chapter Eight ~

Pete left his condo a few minutes early. As a precaution, he set his GPS for Phil's temporary address.

I've been there twice – but both times in the dark with Phil giving turn-by-turn directions. This computerized voice is annoying but I can endure it for the short drive.

This morning he is more aware of the diverse tracts ... condos ... larger homes ... apartments. As he nears his destination he notices that most of the homes were of the same vintage, built just after World War II, to house the hundreds of returning soldiers who settled here. These smaller homes were known as bungalows – sometimes disparagingly called 'matchbox homes.'

Just as the GPS voice barks out "You have reached your destination," he sees Phil standing on the small side porch by the narrow driveway. *He's motioning for me to come in.*

Just inside the door was a small landing which offered two options. Straight ahead, up three steps, was the main floor. To the right were the steps leading to the basement. Taking a few steps down, Phil paused and cautioned "Watch your head ... there's a low clearance right here."

I'm not used to ducking for anything. I'm not that tall.

The entire area was enclosed by dozens of same sized boxes. They were all carefully labeled in bold felt marker and each one clearly identified as ... [Trade Journals] [College Textbooks] [Post Grad Texts] [Doc. Thesis] [Lecture Notes] [Articles]. There were several other boxes with the names of recognized authorities in various Psychological studies – Christian and secular, scholarly and popular, from the past and current. Pete was amazed.

Phil is a reader! There are some names I recognize – many I don't. His psychology library is larger than I've ever seen for one person.

Phil interrupted Pete's thoughts and brought him back to the job at hand. "What do you think?"

"I think you are a true student!"

"But what do you think about our moving project?"

"First ... have you read ALL of these books? Am I right in guessing all these boxes are books?"

"Most of them are books and I've read many ... not all of them. These boxes, my small wardrobe and my computer equipment are all we need to move ... nothing else. So, what size truck do you think we need?"

"We need to talk more about your education. You appear to be a student in the line of Abe Lincoln ... primarily self-educated."

"You won't let that thought go, will you? Alright we can discuss it as we go about our work. Now then, what shall we do about that truck?"

"A small cargo van should do the trick. Even if it takes two trips, it's not that far."

Having decided the truck size decided, and seeing the time, they agree that the next stop will be McDonalds' before they stopped serving breakfast.

As they hustled to Pete's new dream car, he pressed the conversation about Phil's impressive library. "So tell me, how long have you been collecting all those books?"

Slipping into his seat, Phil responded casually "I'm sure you have a huge library too, Pete. Mine is the result of a lifetime pursuit. Many are textbooks from my college and post grad days. For my independent studies, I've purchased several from retired Profs and used book stores. Amazon Marketplace has been another good source. Have you ever shopped them online?"

"Yes, I have ... wide product selection and the prices and service are great! I visit their website often"

As they pulled into McDonalds' parking lot, Pete looked for a spot far away from any other cars to protect his shiny new toy from door dings. "I hope you don't mind a few extra steps this morning."

Phil chuckled "Steps? You haven't seen anything yet! Wait 'til we start lugging all those boxes back up my steps! I remember taking them all down ... with the help of my gracious host. It was a real chore! Hauling them back up will be even worse!"

Once they have their food ... silence prevails. They must have both been hungry because their big breakfasts are gone in a flash.

Because they had not preordered a rental, they have to wait several minutes for the desk clerk to process all the necessary information. Thankfully, it was a Tuesday and there were several small vans available. The wait allowed their breakfasts to settle and gave them time to discuss and decide the best approach in making the move. It also gave Pete time to think...

What comes up from Phil's basement quarters will need to go back down at my place. Oh my, what have I gotten into? Maybe those trips to the gym will pay off now! Phil has been doing some physical work and seems to be in very good shape too. But, we could use some 'younger muscle' right now. Once we have the truck, perhaps we can call one of the dorms and see if a couple guys who stayed on campus will want to earn some quick cash.

As they were leaving Jake's Truck Rental, Peter spoke "You know, Phil, I was just thinking."

"Oh great! Now what?"

"What do you think about hiring a couple of our football players to help us with the heavy lifting and lugging?"

"Sounds great to me! We sure have plenty of 'beef' on our team... if they didn't all go home for the break."

"I think the players are expected to stay on campus with their big awards banquet coming up Friday night. Let's call. I think most of them stay in the Ravine apartments. If they are there, I'm sure two of them would appreciate earning some easy money. Well, easy for them, anyway"

"Do you know their phone number?" Phil asked.

"Here, use my phone. I have the GVSU switchboard on speed dial. Just have the operator connect you with the team's apartment."

A few minutes later, two characters calling themselves Tiny and Tank agreed to meet them at Phil's place in about thirty minutes. Driving there, Pete and Phil had some good laughs about the student's nicknames and made a friendly wager over who will be larger.

GVSU was a perennial preseason favorite for the NCAA Division II National Championship. All of their players, especially the linemen were like walking mountains. They had been rated number one again this year but lost one game during the season and fell short of claiming another title by losing in the second round of the playoffs. The whole team was still in late season shape.

"This little job will be like a combined weight and cardio exercise to help keep our boys in shape. We need to make sure they don't get hurt. Coach would kill us!" Pete cautioned.

Did I really say that? Shortly after Julie's passing I would rebuke anyone who made light of death. Hmmm ... I'm told "time heals all wounds." Time and friends certainly help.

He heard Phil talking but the words weren't penetrating his busy mind. "What? I'm sorry I was lost in my thoughts again. What did you say?"

"I could tell you were either in a different world ... or at least not in this time zone. I said coach is very protective of his team."

"Actually, I was in another decade .... And, yes, he's a great coach and his players love him."

Nearing their destination, Pete spotted their helpers standing by a souped up older model sports car. "I'd say they're ready to tackle this job with gusto!"

"Did you used that football term intentionally, Pete."

"Nope – it just slipped out that way. No pun intended."

"Sure, Pete ... if you say so."

"It's a fact, really."

"Nice car!" Pete and Phil say simultaneously. They could not have been more in unison if they had practiced it.

"Nice truck!" The super jocks responded with obvious delight. "It looks like somethin' a terrorist bomber might use in one of the latest action movies."

"Alright, guys ... a little respect for us older men."

"Hey there, Pete, speak for yourself! I'm NOT that old."

"That's right – you're merely old enough to be their dad I could easily be their grandfather. I get your point."

One of the jocks chided "Maybe we should get started before you two old-timers age anymore? Where's this stuff ya want moved?"

"Okay, guys. I don't think we've actually met. For today you can call me Pete and he's Phi – I mean Jimmy."

"I'm Tank and he's Tiny. I play fullback and he's our All-Conference tackle ... an soon D-two All-American."

"Ease up there, Tank; it's not a done deal yet!" Turning to the OLD GUYS he vowed "I won't hurtcha for calling me Tiny. Just don't call me Timothy ... I hate that name."

Phil spoke first "Timothy is an excellent name with a rich heritage ... nevertheless, Tiny works for me. I value my life!"

"Me too!" Pete exclaimed.

With that settled they proceeded to the basement and Phil warned the younger men "Watch your heads going down these steps. It's a very low clearance – especially for big guys like you."

As they were bending their knees and ducking, one of them said – half joking" Maybe we shoulda brought our helmets."

When Tank reached the bottom of the steps, he blurted out "What's in all'ose boxes? From the markings on'em, it looks like they're books. Why so many?"

"Okay, guys, I have a confession to make ... I'm not Jimmy. That's my middle name. I'm Phillip – or Phil. I took the maintenance job because I was desperate for work. Please help me to keep a low profile until I can get beyond the accusations of theft on campus."

Stunned and amazed, the two athletes simply nod in agreement. They were speechless.

"But ... all those BOOKS ... on PSYCHOLOGY. What's that all about? You a teacher, a professor OR WHAT?"

"When we get done with the move, I'll tell you more – but you must promise to protect my secret until all that messy legal stuff is resolved."

They agreed, verbally this time, and asked where they should start. The group decided that Pete should wheel the boxes to the base of the steps; the jocks could lug them up the steps and to the back of the truck and Phil would arrange them in the truck. That seemed to get maximum use of each man's abilities. Pete sensed that everyone was pleased with his role. They managed to get everything loaded ... books ... clothes ... even Phil's computer and accessories, which he had repacked in the original HP boxes. Surprisingly, the first phase of the move only took about an hour.

Without the extra muscle, I'm certain it would have taken the whole day ... Phil and I would have ached for days ... maybe weeks. Now it's time to take it all to my place. This job is going a lot smoother than I anticipated.

~ Chapter Nine ~

Before pulling out of the driveway, Pete gave Tank and Tiny quick instructions to his place. They roared on close behind him with their CD booming out their favorite hip-hop tunes. The drive took only a few minutes but the change of scenery was most impressive. Pete's condo was in Leisure Valley, a gated community of exquisite homes designed for seniors who enjoyed their privacy ... and could afford it. Although they were condos, from the street they looked more like larger homes. Pete's was at the end of the cul-de-sac, with a substantial yard superbly groomed by the village caretakers.

"Here we are." Pete said with a welcoming tone. "Your new home, Phil!"

"You ... you live here? These ... are mansions!""

"I wouldn't say that but they are comfortable."

As the jocks pulled into the double drive next to the truck, they turned down their CD and somewhat sheepishly said "Sorry! We didn't think about our tunes until we saw the 'Quiet Please' sign next to the 15 MPH speed limit sign."

"That's alright during the daytime ... it's no worse than the caretaker's lawnmowers." Pete replied.

"Are you comparing our music to noisy lawnmowers? Wait don't answer that. I ..."

"Okay, let's go inside."

Phil's obvious astonishment was only increased as they stepped inside and viewed the expansive rooms and the lavish furnishings. The jocks were equally amazed.

"Pete ... this place is LUX-UR-IOUS!

"Yeah, Dr. D ... HOW CAN YOU ...?" The jocks echoed.

"How can I pay for all this? Textbook royalties have been an excellent supplement to my salary. As a tenured professor, I'm paid well too. Speaking engagements pay rather nice honorariums ... it all adds up. Now, let's check out Phil's new living quarters"

When they reached the bottom of the steps, Phil almost fainted. Breathlessly, he asked "Will I be down here alone?"

"That's the plan, Phil. You weren't planning to bring someone with you, were you?"

"No, but it's so huge!" He walked through the spacious great room, featuring a huge fireplace and furnished with a couch, recliners, overstuffed chairs – the works. At the far end was a kitchen and dinette area. A hallway led to a full size bathroom and an enormous bedroom with a cozy little fireplace, two double beds, assorted dressers and a walk-in closet ... that was at least fifteen feet long.

"Oh, yes!" Pete exclaimed "There is an unused workshop that we can convert to a library for all your books."

As they headed back to the steps, Phil was attracted to the west side wall – all windows revealing a beautiful deck with an outside entrance. "Wow! I can enjoy the afternoon sun too. This is FANTASTIC!"

"If it gets to be too much, you have those special blinds

that are between the window panes ... I don't know what you call them – but they are really cool." Pete remarked.

The jocks looked at each other and grinned. "COOL?"

Pete noticed their pleasure at his expense "Okay, so, I'm an antique, right? I could have said 'groovy, far out, rad' or a number of things. What do you guys say?"

Tiny replied "I'm not sure ya wanna know."

From there they went back to work. This time, Pete shoved the boxes to the back of the truck, the jocks then carried them inside and Phil arranged them in orderly stacks for easy distribution – at a later time.

When all of Phil's earthly goods were finally down in the great room, all four men breathed a sigh of relief.

About 30 minutes before they were finished, Pete had ordered two family size pizzas with the works. They came just in time and were nice and hot. He figured that he and Phil would each have a couple slices and the two jocks would devour the rest. He was right.

As they were eating Tank and Tiny reminded Phil that he promised to tell his story. He repeated much of what he had shared with Pete earlier. They listened intently and were visibly touched by all that their friend 'Jimmy ... the Janitor' had endured. Pete even wondered if he saw them wipe away a tear or two. They each gave him a bear hug and a firm slap on the back.

"You guys are tough! I'm glad you were easy on me!"

Yeah, tough on the outside ... Pete practically said it out loud ... but was thankful that he didn't.

When they were finished, Pete reached into his pocket and pulled out his money clip to pay their helpers. They politely refused anything for their work.

"Just come to our awards banquet Friday night and sit at our table ... our dads can't make it. That'd make us proud and be all the pay we want."

"It's a deal, guys! We'll be there!"

Phil reminded them to guard his secret and tried to give them a bear hug ... his arms were too short but they seemed to like it just the same.

Pete and Phil took one last ride in 'the truck' returning it to Jake's. The trip back home was much more relaxing in Pete's new dream ride.

Back home, they were both very tired but that didn't stop them from having a discussion about the jocks. They agreed that their earlier talk about which one would be bigger was totally inappropriate. Both Tank and Tony have HUGE hearts and are both young men they will be honored to call friends and join at their banquet.

They did talk like true football players. Although a bit crude, they did a good job of watching their tongues and keeping it clean. This seemed to please both of the 'older guys.'

This has been quite a day. What will tomorrow bring? The adventure begins! I guess I need to get two tickets for the banquet – tomorrow before they sell out. Phil and I can start building bookshelves in the workshop. We'll have to increase the light in there ... I forgot how dark it was. What was that electricians name? Maybe I need to start another list.

~ Chapter Ten ~

Dr. Michael Wysocki, pompous head of the Psychology Department, was intently reading the owner's manual to his new HP – Envy dv7 laptop computer, when he was startled by a loud knock on his office door. Through the slim vertical window, he recognized two of his problem students.

"Mr. Williams, Mr. Bigler, to what do I owe the honor of your visit ... trouble finding one of my required resources again?"

"No, sir!" Williams replied "We spent a few hours with Jimmy the janitor, whose real name is Phil, and ..."

"Whoa! Stop right there! I'm not interested in any more gossip about that poor fellow ... anyway; I don't think he's the thief." He felt like an outweighed safety trying to stop a huge charging fullback ... a TANK! His voice raised at least two octaves.

"We don't either!" They both roared. "He's a really good guy and has a really shocking story!"

"Story?"

"Don't you know about his history, Dr. Wysocki?" Bigler asked.

"Only that he came from another state where he was fired from his last job. Is there more that you learned? And please ... no gossip."

"It's not gossip. Everything you need to know we heard right from him." Williams reassured.

"So, you think I NEED to know what you learned ... is it that important?"

"OH YEAH! There is a whole lot more about him than most people on campus know, right, Tank?"

"You got that right, Tiny!"

"Okay ... give me an example."

Now they were taking turns responding "He's getting a raw deal! Did you know that he is well educated?"

"How well?"

"Master's Degree and workin' on his Doctorate!"

"Really ... what field?"

"It must be Psychology! His library is huge ... and heavy too. We moved it into the lower level of Dr. Daniels' condo yesterday. There had to be at least forty boxes of books ... all neatly labeled."

"Did you learn what went wrong for him?"

"Yeah ... and it's just as insane as his suspension here at Grand Valley. We need to figger out a way to help him ... NOW!"

Having spilled the story they promised to protect, they insisted that their professor not mention it to anyone. Alone in his office, the professor wondered if they were asking themselves and each other "Did we do the right thing?"

Pacing around his office, his thoughts were racing around in his brain. Then he spoke for no one's ears but his own.

"Yes! We definitely need to help this man. He's had some really bad raps and deserves for someone to come to his aid. Think, brain, think!"

As he was still pondering, another person knocked on his door. This intruder was a well-dressed gentleman who appeared to be in his mid-to-late forties. *Hmm, presents himself well. Carries a laptop ... must be a salesman.*

"I'm sorry, but I don't have time for any sales pitches today! You will need to make an appointment with my secretary ... AFTER the winter break."

"Dr.Wysocki, we do have an appointment! If I arrived too early I can wait out in the hallway until 11:30. That was the time we agreed to meet ... wasn't it? I'm David Daniels from Daniels and Daniels Law Firm."

Oh my, what must he think? It completely slipped my mind. Now I'm the 'absent minded professor.'

"I'm so sorry! Please come on in. I usually don't take appointments during breaks in the university schedule. Please forgive my abrupt demeanor. Your phone call convinced me that we should confer on the recent theft from my office."

"Do you have time for a quick lunch?"

"Absolutely! The time comment earlier was just a ploy to ward off long-winded salesmen. We need to eat anyway, so let's talk over our meal."

"Well, I guess I'm glad I'm not ... a salesman ... but we legal guys can be known to bend an ear at times."

"That's okay. I've developed a new concern for this case. I'm not free to say much at this time ... but I'm certain that our custodian is not the thief. We can spend all the time we need today. Or, is your legal meter running?"

As they were getting into David's shiny new Lexus, he replied "Thanks for your concern about fees, Doctor. We are doing this case pro bono."

"That's very generous! Is there some special reason for this kind gesture? I'm certain Jimmy ... by the way, I learned his name is actually Phil, couldn't afford your services otherwise." *Especially with your rather opulent lifestyle!*

"You've probably made the connection by now. Peter Daniels is our father – Stan's and mine. I'm certain you know him, right?"

"I sure do! There are very few people in this community who don't know Pete. In fact, he is also very well known in the greater academic community. He is quite the guy!" *He seems to have an appetite for life's luxuries too. I guess it runs in the family.*

"Yes he is and an excellent father!"

"I'm sure he is. We are very privileged to have him on our faculty. He has served here for a number of years." *Isn't it about time he retires? How old is he, anyway?*

"Do you like Mexican food? We can go to Los Aztecas. Or, would you prefer something else?"

"Mexican is fine." *I may regret it later ... HEARTBURN!*

So ... it was Mexican. The place was noisy but they agreed that it would drown out their conversation from any other guests who might want to eavesdrop.

Once they had placed their order, Dr. Wysocki restarted the dialog. "So, how did Phil and your father become friends? Are they close?

"If you know dad, he's very social. Since we lost mom, he's had a hard time adjusting to being with couples. He feels kinda like a misfit these days."

"Do you know Phil ... have you met him?"

"Not yet. Stan and I are supposed to be meeting with him and dad in a couple days. Why do you ask?"

"He's an enigma ... a mystery. There's more to that man than most of us have seen. It's really strange and I'm just now starting to get a glimpse into his story."

"Is it good?"

"It's like something you might read in one of those sappy novels about a poor man making it or a rich man failing. All I can say is, if it's true, it feels more like fiction."

"You know what they say 'Truth can be stranger than fiction.' What have you heard?"

"I'm not at liberty to divulge my sources or tell you all I know, but I believe he is a good man and got a bum rap!"

"We do too, Dr. Wysocki. That's why we intend to see that he is exonerated of any charges and restored to the good graces of the University. That includes all missed pay and resumption of his employment."

"That is the very least that he deserves! He is totally overqualified for the menial work he has been doing and should be considered for a staff position or a teaching fellowship here."

"Wow! You must have received some information that has made you so optimistic about his potential."

"It's more than just potential ... he's almost there already ... ON HIS OWN!"

"What ... where?"

"You obviously haven't discussed this with your father yet. He is an educated man ... just a few class hours and a thesis away from his PhD!"

"WOW! Really?"

"Yes! Really!"

"Do you have any idea who took your stuff?"

"No, but I have an idea how to catch them. My grandpa was a cop and my father is a detective. So I have some investigative blood flowing through my veins."

"Ah, a fellow sleuth!"

"You could say that. When I first bought my laptop, I knew it might be a temptation to some shady character. So ... I set a little trap in it ... just for a situation like this."

"Trap?"

"Yes! I placed a phony set on final exam answers in my documents and labeled the file as private and classified."

"You ARE a sleuth! What's next?"

"We bait the trap."

"How?"

"We get the word out that a couple of our athletes are concerned about passing the upcoming Psyc final. I know the perfect duo to pull this off. We just need to inform the faculty and administration about our plan so they will to allow it to work ... without their interference. I'll alert campus security of our plan so they are ready to come on a short notice."

"Sounds like a plan, sir. For now, Daniels and Daniels will just stay out of the way and watch from a distance as the rodent circles the trap."

"Thanks for the lunch, Mr. Daniels; I'll keep you posted on our progress." *He seems like a nice guy in spite of his lavish tastes. I would guess he gets most of his traits from his mother. I wonder what his brother is like.*

Back at his office, Dr. Wysocki immediately picked up his campus directory and looked for the number of his intended cohorts for the big scheme.

Let's see ... U – V – W. Ah, there it is ... Williams ... Billy ... Larry ... Tommy. Tommy? That's right he made it very clear that he prefers to be called Tank – not Tommy.

He quickly punched in the number.

Okay, it's ringing ... Oh great, answering machine ...

"Yes, Mr. Williams, this is Dr. Wysocki. Please call me as soon as you receive this message. We need to talk. Thank you." and he hung up.

Tank and Tiny didn't get back to their apartment until late that evening when they saw the red message light flashing and listened to the recording. It was too late to reach their Prof in his office. Stunned by the message and alarmed by its urgency, they started to imagine all sorts of bad scenarios.

Tank wondered, *did we say too much ... were we out of place ... what does he want to talk about?*

Tiny just paced the floor, not revealing his thoughts.

Both jocks were puzzled and concerned. Now they had to wait until morning to learn what was so important that Dr. Wysocki asked them to call right back.

With busier minds than normal, neither of them slept well. They startled each other at the refrigerator seeking a snack.

After a restless night, they were not ready to face the day – but knew they must. Tank grabbed first turn in the shower and seemed quite refreshed. He quickly put himself together and had a couple Pop Tarts while Tiny took an abbreviated shower – he ran out of hot water. As Tiny finished dressing and had his Breakfast of Champions – Pop Tarts, Tank returned the call to Dr. Wysocki.

He saw The caller's name on his caller ID and answered "Mr. Williams, did you just get my message?"

"Sorry sir, we got in too late ta call you last night."

"I understand ... winter break, right? If you can come right over to my office, I think we can still make the deadline."

"Deadline?"

"I'll explain when you get here – please make haste!"

"Yes, sir!"

Tank hung up, turned to Tiny and said "Let's go!"

"Where?"

"Dr. Wysocki's office. Time's a wastin'!"

The Doctor was waiting for them with a freshly typed note in his hand. It read:

> Two athletes seeking study help for final exams:
>
> 355 Comp. Psyc – Wysocki / 305 Qual. Meth. – Muller
>
> Will pay $20 per hour to qualified tutor.
>
> Please call T. Williams (Number is in Directory)

“Okay, guys, this is the first step in finding the culprit who stole my computer. Get this to the campus paper by noon. I’ll explain when you get back ... hurry!”

The jocks jogged around Zumberge Pond to the Kirkhof Center. They burst into the Lanthorn office, only to learn that the deadline was noon yesterday ... for today’s Thursday edition. So they left the ad with the classified editor to be placed in the next regular issue on Monday January 3. They also learned that students could do a post on the Lanthorn page on Facebook – any time.

Frustrated and curious, they raced back to Dr. Wysocki’s office in Au Sable Hall. As their luck would have it, he was gone and had left a note saying he was off to lunch in the faculty dining facility.

Guessing that they had at least an hour wait for the prof, and starving from their skimpy breakfast, they ambled back to the Kirkhof Center. At the Subway, on the lower level, they both wolfed down a foot long sub, a bag of Nachos and a huge Coke. They each bought a bag of chocolate chip cookies for dessert. Stomachs satisfied, they lumbered back to Dr. Wysocki’s office, lounged in the hallway, and devoured their cookies. Just as they were finishing, the professor to joined their party.

“Well, gentlemen, have we placed an ad for your tutor?”

“Yeah, but it won’t be released til Monday. We kin do a post on the Lanthorn Facebook page. How’s dis gonna work? We aren’t lookin’ for any STUDY HELP!” Tiny bellowed.

“I know ... or I hope not. Here’s the plan ... if you get a call offering to help you study, tell them you already have another person scheduled. If, however, someone tells you they can guarantee a passing grade, arrange to meet them in a public place on campus. They will most likely ask for a large sum of money."

Negotiate the price down and agree to somewhere around a hundred dollars."

"A hunnert bucks that we don't have!" Tank roared.

"You won't need it. I've contacted security and Campus police will be on hand to arrest the snake ... our thief. I've already alerted the administration about our plan. We have their full support."

"Our plan?" Tiny chimed in.

"That's right, 'our plan.' You two have been recruited to help an innocent man get his life back. That's our battle plan and it will succeed. Money talks, men, money talks!"

Meanwhile, less than a mile away ... just off campus, another battle was raging.

~ Chapter Eleven ~

Yesterday, Wednesday, Phil and Pete went to Standale Lumber and picked up a load of fine red oak 8 foot 1x10 boards and all the necessary materials to complete Phil's new library. They spent the entire day laboring on the project until it was finished to their mutual satisfaction. Phil was accustomed to physical labor – Pete was not. So, Pete suffered through a painful and turbulent night. The physical pain seemed quite trivial compared to his all-consuming heartache. But it did seem to intensify his grief and trigger another flare-up of troublesome doubt.

I've made it through Christmas, our anniversary, visits with family ... here I am now. What's left? Does Phil need me ... or do I need him? Why should I go on living? I've lost my wife ... my soul mate ... the love of my life. My friends avoid me ... even God seems to be ignoring me - leaving me, out in the cold, to die of spiritual pneumonia. I'm a misfit in what once were my normal activities. My heart's stone cold ... my brain is dull ... my prayers seem to bounce off the ceiling ... WHY? Why not end it all here? I can't bear this battle ALONE ...

Suddenly, Phil bursts through the front door all bubbly and excited. "It's a beautiful day out there – cold but beautiful! Oh, Pete, I'm sorry. You alright? You don't look so good."

"It's just a bad day, Phil. I didn't sleep well last night and I'm hurting – really hurting."

"Me too ... after working hard all day on my library."

Oh ... yes, I'm aching too ... but this is a different kind of hurt. It's deeper ... a HEART hurt"

"Do you want to talk about it, Pete?"

"Not right now. I'm just tired and weary ... think I'll just lie down for a little while. Maybe we can talk later."

"Okay, Pete, you don't have to go through this alone. I'm here and we're friends. Friends help each other – just like you're helping me."

"I know and your being here is a help already. I've been going through this for months now. It's not something we can solve in a short conversation."

"Fine. Just let me know when you're ready."

Pete trudged off to his bedroom and Phil slipped quietly down to his new living quarters. Stillness enveloped the whole place but storms of doubt and waves of anxiety flooded Pete's spirit. Exhaustion swept over his body. He collapsed onto his bed and was unconscious in seconds. There he rested for several hours sprawled out on his bed ... still in his robe and slippers.

Semiconscious, he glanced at his bedside clock.

Five o'clock ... how did I get here? I must have been up ... robe and slippers? Did I talk to Phil or was I dreaming? ... Throat's dry ... must have been snoring. Need water ... I'm hungry ... wonder if Phil is home? Maybe we can get something to eat.

Then he heard Phil calling out from the base of the steps "I hear footsteps. Are you up?"

"Yes ... and I could eat a horse!"

"That's not a comment on our choice of eateries, is it?"

"Okay, Phil, you always seem to bring a lighter spirit to the table. Speaking of table – what sounds good to eat?"

"Well ... not a horse! I bet you are thinking breakfast."

"You mean a little horse?"

"No! But I can see you are definitely hungry. Do you have anything in the fridge that we can eat?"

"Not really. Being alone, I usually eat out."

"You can't go dressed like that. Put yourself together while I check the paper for some good coupons. There must be some restaurants that serve breakfast all day. You don't mind using coupons, do you?"

"No. Julie and I used them often. She was very thrifty. In fact, her favorite pastime was shopping the thrift stores."

"Didn't that embarrass you?"

"No. But I frequently let her go without me. She would come home and proudly show me her fantastic deals on brand new clothes. That's where I got most of my casual wear. We could spend the savings on other things."

"Like flashy cars?"

"No. That came after she was gone ... something to take my mind off the loneliness. She was not into flashy."

"Sounds like you came from different backgrounds. That can create balance ... or conflict."

"Initially, it was conflict ... but she won me over very quickly. She was definitely a true helpmate ... just what this brash young man needed. It was balance."

"Okay, mister, go get ready! The longer we wait the bigger the horse ... and I haven't found any coupons for any size horse so far. We may have to pay full price"

"In that case, I'll settle for a cow."

"Good! I see coupons for beef ... roast or fried?"

"I'm thinking steak and eggs. Maybe IHOP?"

"IHOP it is. We have a buy-one-get-one free, right here. I suppose you will want to order their unlimited pancakes as well."

"Easy, man!"

"Why not? It will be your only meal today."

"Yeah, then I can sleep with a bowling ball in my gut."

"I bet you didn't talk to Julie like that."

"No and you're not Julie!"

"True and I don't plan to change – even for an intelligent suave fellow like you."

"Good! We don't want anyone to start talking. Although diversity is the new rule for many universities, I have stricter, straighter, rules for my personal behavior."

"So do I! I knew we would be on the same page there."

"I may be confused on many fronts but I'm crystal clear in my position on this issue. We live in a strange world."

After enjoying breakfast at suppertime, and having more time to chat, they headed home. *The day ended better than it had started. How will tomorrow go?*

Just as he was about to turn on the ten o'clock local Fox news, Pete's cell phone rang. Checking his caller ID, he saw his son's name. "Hello, David, what's up?"

"I didn't wake you up did I, dad?" "No, I was just about to watch the news."

"Do you remember when you watched the eleven o'clock news on WOOD TV8? You would fall asleep half way through and our dog, Bandit, would wake you up when the Johnny Carson theme song started."

"I sure do! That was his signal for bedtime. I'm sure that wasn't why you called. What's on your mind, son?"

"I've got some news that will blow your mind!"

"What makes you think my mind isn't already blown?"

"Don't be too hard on yourself, dad. Stan and I were just talking about how strong you've been since losing mom. It has been hard for all of us – but you have suffered the biggest loss and borne the grief amazingly well.

If you only knew ... "Thanks, son that means a lot to me. I've had a lot of support from family and friends. Now that big news. Do you think I can handle it?"

"Absolutely! I just got a call from Dr. Wysocki and he is in full support of clearing your friend from any part in the theft."

"He is?"

"Yes, in fact he already has a plan set in motion to catch the real culprit. And get this ... he is using two athletes to do the front work. This guy is sharp!"

"You mean sharp for a professor, right?"

"Cut me some slack here, dad! I hope you know that I have great admiration for professors – I just didn't want to be one. No offence intended."

"None taken, son, and I'm proud of you and your brother's accomplishments. These two athletes ... they wouldn't just happen to be football players, would they?"

“Yes. I understand they told Wysocki about Jimmy the janitor. You know him as Phil, right? Their conversation confirmed his suspicions of Phil’s innocence.”

“Those RASCALS! We need to keep this info from Phil. He had sworn them to secrecy, but in the long run, I think they did the right thing. For now let’s just keep it under wraps.”

“So, for now, Stan and I are just waiting in the wings while we give Wysocki’s plan a chance to flush out the guilty party. I’m sure it won’t be a party for them.”

“Do you still want us to meet in your office?”

“Let’s give it a few days to see if the weasel comes out of hiding and takes the bait ... maybe even a week.”

“What bait? What should I tell Phil?”

“The less you both know for now the better. Just tell him that something came up and we can’t meet for about a week.”

“I’m intrigued, son ... are you sure I can’t be in on this little secret? I ... CAN be trusted!”

“Relax, dad, I like this plan and feel like it is the best way to get the job done.”

“Okay, son, I guess I can wait.” *Don’t be surprised if I figure it out on my own. Hmm ... what is this sinister plot?*

~ Chapter Twelve ~

After Thursday evening's supper in the student cafeteria, Tank and Tiny high-tail it back to their apartment. Tank plowed in first, kicks aside a Pizza Hut box, and moved right to their desktop computer.

"Whatsa hurry, Tank?"

"I needa get our post on Facebook so we can catch the punk who's gettin' our friend Phil in trouble."

"What if it's a girl?"

"So she's a girl punk. Whatever, we needa get da word out so we can catch'em."

"How we gonna know if it's the for real crook?"

"Hey! 'Member? ... Dr. Wysocki told us. If they offer to help us study, we tell'em we already got help. I'm thinkin' that would be a girl ... one who likes athletes."

"Don't they all, Tank?"

"Some mor'en others."

"What if it's the purrrdy little red-haired girl that sits in front of the class? If she calls, it's my turn ta talk!"

"Sure thing, Charlie Brown."

"Whatchumean by that?

"You know."

"No, I don't! Whatchumean?"

"Charlie and his secret love fer the little red-haired girl in the Peanuts funnies. Charlie ... the shy little loser. "

"Hows'at fit me?"

"Purr-ficly, dude! Dintchu live in the same neighborhood as Charles Schulz when you were young? I bet he used you fer his model fer Charlie Brown."

"Charlie Brown's been 'round long before I was born. How can he be made after me?"

"Sparkie, isn't that what they called him? He had a great imagination. He just thought him up until you came along. Then he jus' copied what he saw. You hafta admit Charlie looks a lot like you did as a kid."

"Well, sorta ... but I'm no Charlie Brown!"

"We'll see. How we gonna know if it's her?"

"We can look'er up on Facebook!"

"Do you know'er name?"

"Um ... not exactly."

"You mean not at all, right?"

"Well, yeah, I guess so."

"Okay, if you can get'er name and she calls AND gives'er name I'll letcha talk to'er. Whatcha gonna say?"

"Haven't thought about that yet."

"Start thinkin' cuz the post is already live, pal."

"Know what? If she answers our post, we can see her picture right there. I hope she does it on Facebook."

"But you can't talk to'er then."

"It's a start!"

"You NEVER had a girlfriend?"

"Is that so hard ta believe?"

"No ... guess not. But ... I think it's time fer ole Tank to show ya the ropes!"

"So, that's how ya do it ... use ropes? I'd just use my MANLY CHARM!"

"Charm? All tree-hunnert pounds of it, right?"

"Don't forget da other fifty pounds, man!"

"If ya call that charm, Tiny, you got more'n the average dude. I'm gonna enjoy watchin' this."

"Okay then ... just sit back and be amazed! Anybody take the bait yet?"

"Not yet ... it's only been about a half hour."

"C'mon, little red-haired girl. Tiny's waitin' fer ya!"

"See, pal, yer getting' right inta da funny pages and don't even know it."

"So, Tank, are you ... Linus ... Schroeder ... Pig Pen?"

"Watch it there, big boy! Or should I say burger boy?"

"Only one?"

"I know, when you place yer order the server asks how soon da rest of yer party will be arrivin'?"

"So I get hungry ... is that a SIN?"

"I guess it all depends on what you call gluttony. How many burger, fries and shakes can one guy eat and still get under da wire?"

"Huh ... what wire?"

"Oh, never mind!"

"I never do!"

"Fer once we agree on somethin'... Hey, let's look up some of the Profs on Facebook."

As they perused the different faculty home pages, they kept an eye on the notifications icon. They didn't want to miss any responses to their 'study help wanted' post. Each time it turned red, they immediately checked to see if anyone had taken the bait. So far, the only comments were sarcastic remarks about 'dumb athletes' and 'lazy jocks.' Not the kind of response they were seeking. After viewing several boring academic pages, they landed on Dr. Daniels' home page ... with delight and amazement.

"WOW! Look at Dr. Maybe's stuff!" Tank chortled.

"How many friends has he got?"

"Way over a thousan' ... and mostly LADIES!"

"Well, he is single ... uh at least widowed. But that's a bunch. Why so many ... Is'at what's distractin' him?"

"It looks like about half of'um are writers. He mus' be in some big writers' thing."

"Is he a writer, Tank?"

"Yeah, 'member at his condo he mentioned royalties?"

"I dint know royalties were somethin' writers got."

"Wha'd ya think he's talkin' about – kings and queens?"

"No! I just dint know!"

"Sorry, Tiny, I sometimes ferget that yer an 'art major' and don't need to know everything us real students do."

"Communications – a real student ... my ... uh ... foot!"

"What's the matter, Tiny ... swearin' off swearin'?"

"Just cuttin' back. It's more sophisticated, ya know?"

"Cuttin' back on a few pounds might help ya too."

"Hey! Coach wants me heavy ... as long as I can hold my own on the line ... and uh ... can get in on the quarterback when I play defense."

"How's 'at workin' fer ya, Mr. All-Conference?"

"I need to knock off about a half a second on my 40's."

"I thought you were still in your 20's, man, what gives?"

"Okay, smarty pants, ya know what I mean ... or don't you sissified ball carriers hafta do sprints 'ese days?"

"Oh yeah, and we need to be faster."

"What? So ya won't be tackled and git hurt."

"So when you miss yer block we can still pick up a few yards. Know what I mean, Timmy?"

"Now you crossed the line! Dem's fightin' words!"

"So Whatcha gonna do – flag me fer off-sides?"

"Keep it up and you'll find ... wait I think we got a comment on our post. The notification light's red."

"Yeah, it is and we have a comment! Come to papa, sucka."

"Is it the little red-haired girl? Le'me see!"

"No – but it IS a girl who wants to help."

"Is she cute? C'mon move over so I kin see!"

"Ya 'member what we were told to do if dis happened? We don't wanna mess up ... trap first – ladies next."

“Okay, now what da we do, Tank?”

“I’m thinkin’ we can message’er and giv’er a stall.”

“Ya mean like a long count to draw’er off-side?”

“More like a ‘time-out’ to let’er think we are considerin’ several people fer da job.”

“Then what?”

“We delete’er comment so the bait’s still fresh.”

“Ya can do that?”

“Easy as a fullback line plunge! That’s with a block.”

“Pickin’ on the linemen agin, Tank?”

“Not if dey execute da block accordin’ to da plans.”

“Okay, let’s do it.”

They quickly dispatched the first respondent and moved back to scoping out Dr. Daniels’ home page.

“I don’t know what it is about him ... but he’s got a pile of chicks as friends! Some are pretty hot! Any ideas how he does it? What’s ‘is secret?”

“Yer askin’ me ... yer da Don Juan on DIS campus!”

“Whoops ... sorry! I was just thinkin’ out loud.”

“Obviously ... but I don’t have a clue.”

Intrigued by their seventy year old professor’s popularity on Facebook, they lost track of time – but they had no more bites on their bait.

As they were logging off, Tiny said “Doncha feel kinda like a fisherman or trapper or even ... a detective?”

~ Chapter Thirteen ~

David Daniels punched in the security code, waited for the gate to open and pulled into the law firm's private parking lot just after eight o'clock. He glided into his personal spot next to Stan's new Beemer. As he entered the office, he found Stan deeply engrossed in researching one of their active case files.

"Hey, Stan, have you been here long?"

"Yeah, I woke up early with some questions about the Maxwell case and decided to verify my suspicions. I was right. Some of these testimonies contradict each other."

"We thought there was something more that we were missing upon casual review. What did you find?"

"According to the plaintiff's witnesses, our accuser was in several different places at the same time."

"We can safely assume that they don't have multiple personalities. Even if he did, he'd have only one body."

"Brilliant deduction, Watson. It sounds like you need more coffee. There's a fresh pot in the break room."

"Thanks! How long have you been here?"

"I don't know. What time is it?"

"Eight fifteen, why?"

"Then I guess I've been here about three hours."

"Three hours! How much sleep did you get?"

"Not enough, but you know me ... and my dedication."

"Yes, I do Stan and you're the best."

"Once you've had your coffee, you're tops at what you do too, brother."

"Mentioning coffee ... this stuff's great! What brand?"

"It's something new from your friends over at Starbucks. It's made from Arabica beans ... has a bolder, less bitter flavor but is low in caffeine. So, I guess, you'll have to drink several cups for the same effect as your regular stuff."

"You know me and coffee. I can do it. Before I forget, I have some interesting news about our case with dad's friend. I met with Dr. Wysocki, whose items were stolen, and he is certain that our man is innocent."

"How so?"

"The two football players, who helped with his move, spilled the beans about his background and education."

"Background ... education?"

"Yes, he is a well-educated man who is within reach of his doctorate. They learned this when they helped him move, saw all of his books and started to ask questions. They were sworn to secrecy but thought the facts were too important to hide. When they told Dr. Wysocki, it confirmed his thinking about Phil – who he had only known as Jimmy the janitor. He had booby trapped his computer just in case it got into the wrong hands."

"Clever! What kind of trap?"

"The best."

"Best?"

"Yes, he created a bogus document labeled something like 'Final exam answers' and placed in a file labeled 'personal and confidential.' Of course, all the answers were incorrect and would serve as bait for the clueless thief. It appears that he suspected anyone who might steal it would be after content more than hardware."

"That's a good one, alright. How does he hope to attract the thief to the trap?"

"He is placing an ad in the campus paper, and one of the football players made a similar post on his Facebook page. Both of these are seeking help 'studying' for their upcoming exams. They offer to pay for help and direct any respondents to call T. Williams, who made the post."

"How does he propose to find the thief by asking for study help? Won't he get other students expecting to earn some honest money?"

"He has provisions for that possibility as well. He thinks the thief will offer a guaranteed good grade for a lump sum. A public location will be arranged for the transfer – but the crook will be met by the police ... not cash."

"You're right, bro, this prof is sharp!"

"He thinks it's in his blood. His father and grandfather were both involved in law enforcement."

"And ... he's a psychology professor?"

"Yes, but something tells me he has aspirations for a change in the near future."

With that open-ended statement, David went to his office and relished the thought of leaving his brother to wonder. Neither of them stayed in the office very long since they both had plans for New Year's Eve.

Meanwhile back at the condo, Pete and Phil were busy discussing breakfast plans and their activities for the day.

“Where would you like to eat, Pete? We’ll most likely have a sizable dinner tonight at the awards banquet.”

“For what the tickets cost, I would hope so!”

“Were they expensive?”

“You tell me ... a hundred dollars a plate!”

“How many plates did you buy?”

“Well, that is per person ... and we don’t get to keep the plates. That’s just a classy way to say that you’re going to pay dearly for this.”

“I know. I was just playing the uncouth janitor. It’s a role I became rather proficient at, don’t you think?”

“I sure do! You had us all fooled for some time there. I did wonder if you were hiding your real self from us.”

“What made you suspicious?”

“Your responses to my notes to ‘Jimmy’ were not typical of someone in your profession. Your grammar ... your handwriting ... they were just too perfect.”

“Wait a minute – weren’t we just talking about food? I ask again ... where shall we eat?”

“Somewhere we can get just enough to tide us over until that big supper. Does it seem strange to you having a banquet on New Year’s Eve?”

Phil agreed and said no more. So, it was IHOP again, where they both ordered the ‘lite breakfast’ and decided it would be exactly enough. As they waited for their food, Pete broke the silence with some news he wasn’t quite certain how to deliver.

"Um ... I got a call from my son, David, and it seems they won't be able to meet with us for a week or so."

"Oh, did he say why?"

"Only that something came up with one of their cases that required some immediate attention ... AND that they needed more time to gather some vital info on your case."

"They aren't having second thoughts are they? If so, I can certainly understand. According to the local news, they have some really high profile cases going right now."

"So, you've noticed that too? NO, NO, NO, they will not back out on you! They'll stick with you until you are completely exonerated. That's how they operate. AND ... if they didn't, I would make sure they did in your case."

"How long have they had their law firm?"

"Ever since they completed their education and became certified. Goodness, it's approaching twenty years now."

"What prompted them to choose that field?"

"You mean as opposed to farming the fields?"

"NO! Let's say instead of education ... like you?"

"First of all, they always considered themselves to be individuals ... NOT like me. They were self-starters and not carbon copies of anyone – especially me."

"Did that bother you?"

"Not at all. I was proud of their individuality."

"Now you can be proud of their accomplishments."

"I am, and I've told them many times."

"Did your father express his love and admiration?"

"No, it was not considered manly back then."

"My father did ... but I think it was an attempt to be a better man than his dad – who didn't. I'm guessing that my grandfather grew up in the same era as your father."

"Sounds reasonable – given the difference in our ages. Many things have changed in the last few generations."

"Especially things like decency, respect, loyalty, integrity and commitment ... did I forget anything?"

"I can't think of anything else – but if it's good ... it probably won't last another generation. I'm sounding like an old crank now. We better change the subject before I get up on my soapbox."

"Soapbox?"

"Oh sorry, that's a figure of speech from my father's time. Didn't you ever hear your grandfather talk about zealots getting on their soapboxes?"

"I hardly knew my grandpa."

"I didn't either. My mother's dad died in an accident when she was just in her teens. My other grandpa was not so grand. What I heard about him was not even good. I'm told he was quite the reprobate... just another bad apple from the family tree."

"I haven't heard much about my ancestors. Maybe that's a good thing ... better than knowing a lot of bad stuff."

"You've got that right, Phil."

"Weren't we going to change the subject? Let's talk about tonight. Did you get any info on the dress code for the evening? It's not formal, is it?"

"Oh no! These are football players and I doubt they make tuxedos large enough for them. Dress suits are fine."

"Good! My brothers took me to their local men's store and bought me a classy new one. My old one is probably out of style – if it even fits."

"That's a timely purchase. You'll feel right at home. Are your brothers still after you to manage a hardware store?"

"They've given it a rest ... for now ... at least until I get past my legal battle. After that is resolved, I may have to break the news to them – gradually."

"What news?"

"I'm thinking that the Lord has something for me here in Michigan. What? ... I don't know. It's just a hunch."

"I hope so, Phil! I believe in you. You're gifted ... you have great potential."

"Okay, Pete, who gifted me?"

"Ease up there, pal, I'm not quite ready to have that talk. Please ... give me a little slack. Okay?"

"Okay, but we don't have forever you know – at least not in our present state."

"I'm assuming you're not talking about Michigan."

"You're assuming right. I think you know what I mean."

"Yes, I do and your patience gives me the assurance that when I do spill my guts, you will be the victim."

"Not a victim, Pete. We're friends and as friends we help each other. When you are ready ... I'm here."

"You don't know how much that means to me, friend!"

"I already owe you for giving me a place to live. But, I don't intend to overstay my welcome."

"Let's not talk about how long you will stay. Let's take one day at a time. Now then, what are your thoughts about tonight's banquet?"

"Sounds like a great time with plenty of tasty food – but we're going to look like dwarfs among those monsters."

"Wasn't there a Smiley? That's me. You can be Sleepy."

"Ouch! Touché! You're not letting me forget that, are you? How do you think our boys will look in suits?"

"LARGE!"

"You've got that right!"

"Well, I guess we had better head for home. We'll need to get ready for the big shindig before long."

As they were leaving the IHOP, Pete left a very generous tip explaining "We were taking up one of Nicole's prime tables for quite a long time. She may have been able to serve another customer and receive two tips in that time."

"You don't have to explain to me, Pete. I know you're a good man and generous with all you possess."

"The question is whether I'm good enough."

"Don't go there friend ... unless you're ready for the talk!"

"Let's see what tomorrow brings. It's New Year's Day, you know."

"I would like to have you go to my church sometime ... soon ... when you're ready."

"We'll see ..."

~ Chapter Fourteen ~

Back home, the two gentlemen started setting out their clothes for the awards banquet. Pete chose his favorite suit, the navy blue, Armani, 100% virgin wool, single breasted, comfort edition. He added a pure white silk shirt, a Dirosa silk tie, black socks, and brushed calfskin, side buckled shoes. No one was going to outshine Dr. Daniels tonight ... AND no one needed to know that he had purchased all of these items at a high class men's store in Chicago that was going out of business.

Still in his casual attire, Pete ventured downstairs and saw Phil admiring his only decent dress outfit. One that his brothers bought for him when he was back home. It was certainly suitable ... but not ostentatious like Pete's. But, it didn't cost him a couple thousand dollars either. *Dave Ramsey would be proud of Phil ... and I know he isn't trying to impress anyone. He's already told me that all he wants to do is blend in with the other average Joes who are there to show their support for the team. No doubt, the high rollers will be impressed by my expensive threads – but he's not ready for that scene yet. He doesn't seem to be a guy who would desire center stage. After all, he has been working as a janitor.*

"Hey, Pete, is it time to get dressed in our fancy duds?"

"We probably want to get there early. So I'd say yes."

Once they were all spiffed up, Phil commented about Pete's wardrobe. "How many outfits do you have in your closet like that one? You look like Mr. Senior G Q!"

"This is it, Phil, and I practically stole it."

"No offense, Pete, but I would rather not hear you talk like that ... if you know what I mean."

"Sorry, pal, I wasn't thinking about your situation. I have a problem with speaking THEN thinking. It has caused me trouble more than once. I'll try to be more thoughtful from now on."

"Thanks! I need to get over being so sensitive about it ... but this whole mess has me concerned to the point of not being myself lately. Does that make sense to you?"

"It does – but I can't say that I've noticed any change in your behavior. You have been handling it very well."

"I've tried to keep it inside and that just makes matters worse. I need to exercise my faith more in God and less in myself. Sorry ... I'm preaching at myself – not you."

"I fully understand. Believe it or not ... I fully agree! My comment ... the hasty one ... I was trying to say that these clothes I'm wearing ... all bought on clearance. Oh sure, I still paid too much. I felt like they would last a long time and would be nice to wear when I'm on speaking and book tours – okay I wanted to spoil myself. So there."

"They look great, Pete! Wear them guilt free."

~

Meanwhile, back at their Ravines apartment, Tank and Tiny were also getting ready for the banquet.

"Now remember, Tiny, we are going to be with some really important people tonight. They're honoring our team but they will be looking for ways to impress each other as well. So watch your words!"

"Hey man, gimme a break! I already told you that I've cut back on my swearin'! What more kin I do?"

"That's very good. But I'm talking about grammar not language. If you can ... get rid of your lazy tongue. That's okay when it's just us guys – but in this crowd ... you need to enunciate."

"Who ate what?"

"Okay. Pronounce your words clearly. Not 'gimme' or 'gonna' – but 'give me' and 'going to' ... just like when we interact with our Profs. Can you do that?"

"I'll try ... but I'm gonna need help!"

"Start right now! Say that again."

"That again."

"No! What you just said before ... I'll try ..."

"Oh! I'll try ... but I'm gonna ... whoops ... going to need some help."

"That's better!"

"I'm serious, Tank, I'll need help. As you said earlier, I'm an art major. You're the communications major. So you need to help me."

"You're doing better already! Just keep your mind on what you're saying. Speak slowly if that will help. You know many deep thinkers speak slowly. It makes their listeners think they are pondering every word so as to be profound. But don't get too carried away with it."

“Okay, Tank, you lead I’ll follow. Just the opposite of what we do on the football field, right? I throw the blocks so you ball carriers can sneak through the holes.”

“Well, ideally that’s how it’s supposed to work. But sometimes you just slow them down and your pal Tank has to plow through or over them. Now then, back to the subject at hand. You stick by me and let me do most of the talking. As you hear me, you will be able to pick up on it.”

“Sounds good. How does this suit look on me?”

“Great but don’t try to bend over too far.”

“Are - you - saying - what - I - think - you’re - saying?”

“Yes and you asked that question perfectly ... slowly and perfectly.”

“This is my only suit that fits ... well almost fits.”

“Maybe I’ll have to lead from behind.”

“Is it that bad?”

“You shouldn’t take any chances!”

“Come to think of it, I did gain a few pounds since I got this suit. It’s only about a year old.”

“The problem, pal, is not how many months but how many pounds.”

“I’d say about twenty.”

“Bingo! That’s enough.”

“Guess I need to be careful getting in and out of the car.”

“You’ll need to be careful doing everything – even breathing. Don’t be nervous ... just be careful.”

"Sure, Tank, that's easy for you to say. You don't need to walk around in my pants."

"If I did, I'd have another problem ... keeping them up."

Both of the jocks expressed relief that Tiny was able to ease in and out of the car. It wasn't a pretty sight – but he made it. Thankfully, no one seemed to notice.

~

The jocks and the gentlemen arrived at the banquet at about the same time. This allowed the two athletes to see Pete's shiny new Electric Blue 2011 Lexus CT200h. Stepping out of it, he looked like an investment tycoon. Their jaws dropped in amazement. Pete just grinned.

Since their arrival was so timely, they were able to walk in together and find their table before stopping to talk with other guests. Their place cards were on a table front and center just across from the head table. Tank said that he expected it was because the boosters would be giving Tiny some special honor. So far – so good. At least he would not need to walk far to the podium.

As they mingled throughout the crowd, they recognized local TV News people, city council members, prominent business people, and anyone who was important or thought they were. There was a bevy of fat cats and the usual social climbers. But the true heroes of the night, THE TEAM, were there in full force. The foursome soon decided this was the place to be tonight ... and there they were in the best seats in the house.

After a time of handshakes and bear hugs, the moderator called for attention and introduced the minister of the oldest downtown church for the invocation. After the prayer, if that's what it was, Pete shot a puzzled glance at Phil and received a similar return expression. The jocks appeared to be oblivious to the concern their guests were experiencing.

Pete noticed that the servers were not only prompt and efficient ... some were very attractive. That may call for further investigation ... later. As he was enjoying one of the best prime rib dinners he'd tasted in ages, his thought turned to the two young friends who had invited him. *What's their religious background? How could I become concerned with their spiritual condition when my own life is in shambles? That minister ... who was he 'praying' to? 'God, our father-mother'? 'Thou great spirit of the wind'? This doesn't sound like Phil's pastor. Phil talks about God the Father, Jesus the Son, and the Holy Spirit. That's more like it. Not all that hocus pocus stuff! What is this world coming to? What am I ...*

"Pete, Pete, are you with us?

He heard the words ... but it took a moment to register.

"I think he's coming in for landing now, guys." Phil said "You do know, of course, that he is our renowned and highly esteemed Doctor of Philosophy. His mind travels to thought plains we can only read about in the annals of greats like Plato, Aristotle, and Xenophon."

"Zenno who?" Tiny blurted. Tank pinched his own lips together signaling for Tiny to shut up.

Now that they had Pete's attention, he realized the speaker at the microphone was leading into the awards presentations. *Already? How much did I miss? How long was I off in my own little world? What's happening to me?*

Then he heard it ... both Tank and Tiny were named NCAA Division II ... First Team All-Americans. The crowd stood and gave them a thundering ovation as they lumbered up to the podium.

The two honorees stood like trees behind the very small podium. It was just tall enough to hide Tiny's nervous knees. There they were, like two mountains, arms around each other's shoulders, a sight to behold.

Tank spoke first and was visibly astonished. "I knew my pal here was a sure thing for this recognition ... but I'm amazed to be standing here with him"

He went on to thank his parents for their dedication and for instilling in him solid values and a strong work ethic. Explaining that they were unable to attend and pointing to his table, he thanked his new friends and special guest for standing in for them. He thanked his coaches, his team, and the GVSU Booster's Club.

"I will do my best to live up to this honor and bring the National Championship back to Grand Valley next year!"

This brought a resounding cheer from the audience and a lot of whoops and hollers from the team. Just like the players, the alumni jocks joined right in ... reliving their glory days.

When it was Tiny's turn to speak, he felt Tank's strong hand on his shoulder ... supporting his large frame. He started "What he said ..." This brought a hearty laugh from the crowd and seemed to give him the confidence to continue. He did repeat much of what Tank said but also thanked his parents for their sacrificial investment in groceries. This seemed to strike a humorous note with the crowd and brought more laughter. To this he replied "I'm serious! I didn't get this big on a skimpy food budget!"

He finished well and Tank gave him a congratulatory slap on the shoulder. Then as if rehearsed, they both pointed an index finger toward the ceiling and loudly ... unapologetically said "We want to thank the Good Lord above for His many blessings!"

Pete was stunned. W*hat is this? I'm surrounded! But it feels kinda good.*

He looked over at Phil who was smiling ... but tears were running down his cheeks.

On the way home they both were quiet until Pete broke the silence. "What a night!"

"Yes it was, friend. Yes it was."

"May I ask you a personal question, Phil?"

"Certainly ... if it's not too difficult."

"I've been curious for some time. You are a real human, aren't you? You're not one of those ...um ... angels? I didn't see any wings but ..."

"No! I'm as much flesh and blood as you are; and I'm not sure angels need wings. What gave you that idea?"

"I guess the way you came on the scene at a time when I needed someone and let me help you ... which is really helping me the most. It seemed too coincidental."

"People can do that too, Pete, if they're willing."

"True ... that's a mighty big if!"

~ Chapter Fifteen ~

Meanwhile, back at the banquet hall, Tank and Tiny stayed and enjoyed celebrating with their teammates. It gave them a chance to thank each member of the squad for all they had done to make this a memorable night.

Once the crowd had cleared out, they were left with their inner circle of friends. Crusher, an up and coming new defensive tackle, shot a quick barb at the two new All Americans.

"So, what's this thing ... hangin' out with the old coots?"

Tiny took immediate offense to his making fun of his new friends and comrades. "Hey, they may be older than we are, but dey're good guys, ain't that right Tank?"

"Yeah ... like another dad and grandpa ... who both have time for us and are pullin' for us. You ought'a get to know'em. Dr. Daniels is one class act ... flashy clothes ... hot car ... lots'a chicks followin' him on Facebook ... the whole enchilada! Jimmy is great too, you'll see."

The small group all responded together on that point.

"Oh yeah?"

"Yeah! And dey actually cares about us student peons."

One of the cynics shot back "We'll see where dey are when we really need'em. Dat's da true test!"

"Yes, we will!" Tank responded "Yes we will!"

When the cleanup crew started stacking chairs and rolling the round tables into a back hallway, the guys took the cue and decided it was time to move on. Stepping outside, they didn't linger long in the frigid December air; but parted ways and headed back to their apartments.

Rumbling along in Tank's street rod, Tiny asked "Do you really think they bought what we said about our friends?"

"It's gonna take some time for them to come around. But I think they will. Take my word for it."

"Yeah. What ya said about'em ... did ya mean it?"

"For sure! Now ... they both do have some issues."

"What kinda issues?"

"Well ... I think Dr. D. is dealin' with more'n just grief. He seems to be having some security issues."

"How kin ya tell that?"

"His macho man image. You know, clothes, car ... all that stuff. He's coverin' somethin' up. I guarantee it."

"Yeah, I wondered about dat too. He wasn't dat way when 'is wife was still alive. What's 'is problem?"

"I don't really know and I'm not sure we can help him either. So I guess we hafta just watch and wait."

"Dat'sa hard part. What about Jimmy ... er Phil? I saw you called him Jimmy wid da guys. Why?"

"That's how they know'im. So we need to help protect his secret until he's cleared. His problem seems to be dealin' with a reputation that doesn't fit his true character and it's eating him up. That is somethin' we can help with. All we hafta do is catch the real thief."

"All ... ?! Dat seems like a purdy big job to me!"

"We can do it. Who knows, we may have someone takin' the bait right now."

As they walked in the door, they both rushed to their computer to check for activity on their post. There were seven comments ... none were the culprit. Several were more snide remarks about dumb jocks that were just in school for their athletic ability. That hurt almost as much as a low block or illegal tackle, but they had learned to get up and keep on going. Maybe tomorrow ...

Tank didn't sleep much, due partly to excitement over the night's honors, partly to curiosity surrounding his new friends' challenges, but mostly to his wanting to catch the thief. It was about two in the morning, when he and Tiny collided in the dark, that he learned that they were both having trouble sleeping.

Food was calling. They hauled out some leftover pizza and polished it off in no time. Leftovers weren't that common in their place – but they came in handy tonight. Hunger pangs satisfied, Tank decided to go back to bed. Soon he heard his pal shuffle off to his room. He was snoring within a few minutes. Moments later, Tank was out too.

They both slept in past nine and were still dragging around at ten. Every few minutes one of them went to the computer to check the trap. Nothing!

It was Saturday, winter break and their schedules were free from any pressing commitments – so they relaxed and watched a couple bowl games on TV.

Yeah ... this is the life, Tank! Yeah ... but you know won't last ... Dr. Wysocki's big exam is a comin'!

Tiny waited for a commercial break and asked Tank how well he knew their new friends.

"I first met Dr. D. last year, as a sophomore, when I took his Intro to Philosophy class. He'd just lost his wife to that heart attack. He seemed to be alright then – but as time passed, he seemed to become gloomy ... detached and ... frequently missed classes or dismissed them early. He'd changed ... and not for the better. He seemed to be lost and alone ... really sad. Then a few class jerks had to start calling him names because of his missing class or bein' late. It was UGLY! But he never took it out on us even though it was clear that he was a hurtin' man."

"What didya do?"

"Nothing ... I was just a student – a sophomore at that. I didn't know what to do. Then he seemed to rally ... new car ... new clothes ... a new bounce in his step. I learned he'd met a new lady friend and it seemed quite serious."

"Didya meet her?"

"Oh ... no. It was not that widely known. The person who told me swore me to secrecy."

"Who told ya?"

"That's part of the secret. I can't say."

"Or won't!"

"No ... can't! I promised to keep it confidential – so it it's confidential. His new romance lasted 'til mid-September. Then he seemed to slip back some. Not all the way ... he seemed more determined now. We'll have to have our talk about Phil later. We've got more hits on our post."

"Is it the little red-haired girl?"

"Settle, Charlie!" *Touché! Gotcha, big boy!*

~ Chapter Sixteen ~

New Year's Day 2011 arrived with no fanfare ... it just came. As they were eating a light breakfast, Phil cocked his head and grinned "So, did you really think I might be an angel? You knew me better than that, didn't you?"

"I thought I knew you but ..."

"You said my circumstances made you suspicious. How so? What about me didn't seem to fit?"

"Well ... you arrived in town alone. You got a job where you were in frequent contact with me and got to know me – just when I needed help. Then we meet on campus one dark night and YOU need MY help. Don't those things seem a bit contrived to you?"

"When you put it that way ... I see your point. Relax, Pete, I am just a human. On the other hand, I do believe the Lord brought us together for a reason."

"I do too, Phil ... and I feel like the time has come for our long delayed discussion about my issues ... problems."

"Are you sure, Pete? I don't want to rush you."

"I'm ready! My story could go on for days and I don't want to put it off any longer. Let's get started."

As they headed down to Phil's new library he said "Okay. Where do we start?"

"My parents. Some important background." Pete offered.

"Then, let's hear it."

"They weren't serious church going people. As I said earlier, my mom's parents had both died by the time she was fourteen. My dad's folks had split up. His dad was a womanizing alcoholic and his mom had her own beauty shop in their home. My dad had a sister who, from all reports, was a saint. Dad was not!"

"So, how does this affect your story?"

"My guess is that I was conceived in the back seat of an old Chevy by two unmarried drunks." Pete asserted.

"What makes you say that?"

"Their lifestyles and the fact that I was born – full term – seven months and twenty-two days after their wedding."

"That could cause a person to wonder."

"Especially this person." Pete shuddered.

"In your early years, you didn't know all this, right?"

"Right, but it didn't take long to sense that I hampered their social lives. I was an only child and the only one to disrupt their party life. They showed their frustration in how they disciplined ... impatient and angry. I grew up a lonely and insecure child."

"I would never have believed that." Phil grinned.

"Things improved later; but through grade school, I was a shy little guy. We moved a lot so I had few friends of my own. Most of the time, I had to play with my parents' friend's kids ... spoiled brats!

I heard somewhere that some of my dad's friends were card-carrying Communists. It didn't surprise me."

"Wow... That's amazing, Pete! Tell me about your moves. Did you have to change schools too?"

"Oh yeah! I went to kindergarten in a large school with several hundred students. We then moved to another area where I attended first and second grade in a one room country school. From there, we moved to Jackson where the grade school I attended had four classes for every grade. I heard rumors that the principal spanked with a rubber hose ... I never found out."

Phil looked up from arranging books. "Four years and three schools? Tell me it got better after that."

"Somewhat. We were back on a farm where I attended another one room country school – grades four through six ... different teacher each year ... different discipline. That community had many activities for families. At one of the regular events, a roller skating party, I always hid in the men's room when they had the ladies' choice. I was really shy and not very comfortable socially. I was invited to Vacation Bible School by my trouble-making neighbor friend ... the last day I 'got saved' I thought."

"You thought ...? What do you mean by that? Those must have been difficult years. Then what ...?"
"The decision didn't make any difference. We moved back to Jackson and I went to an intermediate school for grades seven and eight. Although it was an older school, it had two gyms, an indoor oval bowled cork track, and an indoor pool. That's when I started to break out of my shell."

"How did you do that?"

"My folks bought this franchise for a wholesale donut bakery and poured their entire life into trying to make it succeed. I had no one to hold me liable for my behavior – well misbehavior. They worked through the nights. I was on my own ... but they left money for my meals."

"Were you bad?"

"In a word ... yes! I hung out with the wrong crowd and took on their ways ... smoked rum soaked Havana cigars at the age of fourteen ... got kicked out of classes ... fights ... all while carrying straight A's in all my classes. Wow ... look at the time! You hungry?"

"We're making good progress with my books. Let's take a lunch break. What sounds good to you?"

Pete stopped unpacking boxes. "You make the call."

"Okay, it's Mickey D's!"

While they ate, their conversation focused on small talk and lighter subjects. Pete was relieved with the change.

~

Back at Phil's library, Pete said "Shouldn't I be reclining on a couch with a counseling meter running for these sessions? Here I am spilling my guts to you ... hope you don't charge by the hour."

Phil chuckled "Don't forget all the time we spent with my story? You're giving me free lodging AND your sons are helping with my case! It's what friends do but your story will receive the same privacy as client's."

"That's reassuring! Are you ready to hear more?"

"Whenever you are. We can keep sorting my books as we talk, right?"

"Absolutely! Let's see ... I was telling you about moving back to Jackson. As I mentioned earlier, my folk's bought a bakery and spent every waking hour making it succeed. That took up all of their time. It worked until their landlord decided to cancel the verbal lease. Having to relocate, they worked day and night bringing their new location up to the rigid local health standards. They also had to buy tens of thousands of donuts a week, from an out of town franchise, to satisfy their customers. This went on until they were able to make their own,"

"How long did they have to do that?"

"Several weeks! Meanwhile ... a local competitor, an 'upstanding church going man,' told most of our larger customers we were going out of business. Now dad had to add damage control to his increasing list of duties. His health broke. He and mom separated for a while ... everything went sour."

"Sounds devastating ... how did they survive?"

"They lost everything owing an additional $10,000. That was a lot of money back in 1955."

"That's a lot of money today!" Phil exclaimed.

"Back then ten dollars would buy a week's groceries for three. Dad tried to work but every job he got the creditors would garnishee his paycheck. Finally we had to leave Jackson with little more than the clothes on our backs."

"Where did you go?"

"We moved back to Grand Rapids. I didn't want to leave because I had a special girlfriend. Of course I didn't know how bad the situation was until months later. When dad considered filing bankruptcy, his sister – the saint – got in his face and reminded him of his moral obligation. Remember those words?"

"I sure do ... and it's always the right thing to do!"

"Well, before moving to Grand Rapids, mom and dad got back together and met with the pastor of the church where I went to that VBS. This was in a small town about forty miles away. He strongly encouraged them to get in a church that preached the Word. Dad had been attending meetings with a group we would call a cult ... so he could play on their basketball team. I guess you could say his priorities were way out of whack."

"I guess so!"

Pete sighed. "Well, their business failure was a serious wakeup call for him and the change was dramatic. In a spiral notebook, he made a list of all of his creditors and what he owed each of them. He got a fulltime job in a factory and worked an additional thirty hours a week as a locker-room attendant at the YMCA. Mom got a fulltime job at a local pharmaceutical supplier."

"How did you do with these new arrangements?"

Pete smiled. "It was different, this time. I was aware of their dilemma. They sent money orders to each of their creditors – with no return address to avoid having some-one come after their whole debt. In five years, making these payments and using a strict cash budget, they were debt free. They paid cash for everything. They were able to buy a house on a land contract."

"There you were alone again!"

"True, but I always had money for meals and never lacked for clothes ... thanks to mom and thrift stores."

"What about family life ... church?"

"We had our weekends together as a family and attended church three times a week. I had parents again"

"Did this change your habits?"

Frowning, Pete replied "Not immediately. Again, I found the wrong friends at school. The first three semesters at Creston High, were much like my days in Jackson."

"How so?"

"More fights ... cutting up in class and getting sent to the principal's office. I did quit smoking."

"Was that hard for you?"

"No. I never got hooked and didn't really enjoy it that much. I quit because I was going out for the track team."

"Did you have to change friends when you quit?"

"It's interesting that you ask. My former smoking buddy came up to me one day with a cigarette in his mouth. He took it out and blew smoke in my face and put it back in his mouth. 'So, you've quit smoking ... you a chicken?' That angered me. I took the cigarette out of his mouth and smashed it on his lips – fire first. Without hesitating, I slapped his face with a backhand and asked him 'What did you say?' He was shocked and sulked off. He never bothered me again about smoking."

"I can believe that! What got into you?"

"I wasn't about to let someone intimidate me for quitting an unhealthy habit... especially like that!"

"You referred to your first three semesters at Creston as being a continuation of your Jackson days. So, what happened after that?"

"I got involved in this club."

"Club ... what kind of club?"

"Are you ready for this? It was a Bible club ... sponsored by Youth for Christ."

"What in the world got you involved in a Bible club?"

"So, Phil, don't you see me as a theologian?" he chided.

"Not from what I've heard about your past! So ... what did it take for you to make this major leap?"

"More like WHO, not what."

"Okay, who? Was it a friend?"

"Potentially." Pete responded with a smirk.

Not amused, Phil retorted "Is this turning into a guessing game now? What do you mean by that?"

Enjoying Phil's frustration, Pete said "It was someone I thought could and SHOULD be a friend."

"Why, Pete?"

"Because they had a tremendous personality and exuded a confidence that was just amazing. I found myself drawn to them in ways I could not explain."

"This person ... was it a girl?"

"Bingo!"

"And was she pretty?"

"Beyond words, Phil! Bee-yond words!"

"So, Pete, this is your wife ... uh Julie, right?"

"Oh goodness no! Remember I was in the tenth grade ... sixteen. Julie was five years younger – only eleven. We didn't meet for another seven years; and we both did a lot of living in those years. Our meeting was quite an experience though. But that's another story for another time. What made you think it was her?"

"Well, the way you were so totally enthralled by her."

"I've only told that story a few times ... each time I've had the same response. Maybe I was a bit carried away."

"I think so. You implied that you couldn't describe her. I find that rather surprising for you the wordsmith. After all, you are an award winning author, an accomplished lecturer, and popular conference speaker."

"You flatter me! If all of that is true, it's me now. Back then, I hated to read and couldn't write a simple theme."

"What changed you?"

"Attending the Bible Club became an incredible turning point in my life."

"And ... the girl ... what became of her?"

"That's a mystery I haven't been able to solve to this day. I don't have the faintest clue."

"Now I am confused. What are you saying?"

"I did see her in club a few times but we never sat close enough for me to start a conversation. Believe me ... I really wanted to get acquainted!"

"Oh yeah, I believe you!"

"I saw her in the hallways but we were both hurrying to classes in different parts of the building."

"Like ships passing in the night?"

"Exactly!"

"Did you get her name?"

"I think it was Janice Vander something."

"Imagine that ... a Dutch person in Grand Rapids. You did get to talk with her eventually, right?"

"NO! I didn't! She just vanished. I tried to find someone in our club who knew her. No one could identify her ... no one knew what had become of her. I even checked my yearbooks to see if she was in any of them. Nothing!"

"That certainly qualifies as a mystery to me, Pete."

"You don't suppose she was an ...?"

"An angel?" Phil grinned.

"Yes. You know – to get me on the straight and narrow."

"I really doubt it. The only angels mentioned in the Bible had male names. Now then, as you know, Greek and Roman mythology had goddesses ... I doubt you want to go there." Phil challenged.

"No, but I still haven't given up hope of finding that gal. One way or another ... she was my angel!"

"It sounds like you kept going to the Bible Club anyway. How did it change your life?"

Pete stretched and yawned "That is a very long story, Phil, which will have to wait for another day."

"Can I talk you into going to church with me tomorrow?"

Somewhat amused, Pete countered. "That wasn't even subtle, was it? Let's see what morning brings."

He's only been here a few days and he's already after me. Is this the kind of thing I'm going to have to deal with now?

~ Chapter Seventeen ~

Pete tossed and turned.

Ahh ... sizzling hot bacon and freshly brewed coffee ... is this a dream or what?

He rolled out of his warm cozy bed, quickly put on his slippers and robe, and shuffled toward the stairway to Phil's quarters. "What's cooking down there, man?"

"Exactly what your nose is telling you. C'mon down! It's almost ready and there's enough for two hungry men. How do you like your eggs?"

"Scrambled dry then slathered with butter."

"Slathered?"

"Oh, yeah, that's the way they do it in the South. They LOVE to slather. They spread a thick layer of butter on eggs, biscuits, toast and grits."

"That actually sounds pretty good. I may try it myself."

"They do things differently down there ... like grape jelly on their sausage, egg and cheese McMuffins."

"That's strange!"

"You should try it. I eat mine that way all the time now." Pausing briefly he asked "What time is it anyway?"

"A bit after six, why?

"I thought it seemed early for a Sunday morning."

"Yes, Sunday morning. That's my whole point. Let's eat then we can talk about it."

The discussion didn't wait until they had finished eating.

Pete took his first bite, savored it and swallowed "This is a great breakfast, Phil! I'm assuming you want to talk about church, right?"

"Yeah, CHURCH, are you game to try it this morning?"

"Maybe ... but why so early? It doesn't start until about eleven, does it?"

They continued to talk as they ate.

"We have two morning services ... a traditional one – my style – at eight-thirty and a contemporary one for the kids at ten-thirty."

"And you had me pegged for the traditional, right?"

"Well, the contemporary is even a bit too hip for me!"

"Hip?"

"Hip ... hip hop ... whatever."

"Tell me about the traditional one."

"Most of those who attend are seniors ... balding or gray haired men and blue haired ladies."

"Sounds like I would fit right in."

"I agree, and I don't stand out as much there as I would with the younger set."

"What are the services like?"

"Choir ... song leader ... we sing from both the hymnal and off the wall ... mostly familiar songs and hymns."

"Sounds like my style. The preaching?"

"Our pastor is a teacher ... a verse-by-verse expositor."

"That's good. I don't like a lot of shouting and drama. How do we dress?"

"We're quite informal ... some of the men still wear suits. I prefer comfortable dress slacks and a sweater."

"Any Cardigans?"

"Maybe, but I don't think we have any Mr. Rogers types. We do have many kindly older men though."

They finished eating ... polishing off everything Phil had cooked. They were both happily stuffed. After clearing the table and loading the dishwasher, they agreed to leave for church by eight o'clock.

"Church is just a few minutes away, but I'd like time to introduce you to some of my friends."

Pete was a bit apprehensive about meeting these new church folk but went along with Phil's plan. He liked the thought of having time to scan the Grand Rapids Press before getting himself ready ... for church.

It's been a time ... hope I don't do something embarrassing like drop the offering plate. They still 'pass the plates,' don't they? It's strangely comforting that Phil's church sounds a lot like those I've enjoyed over the years. Maybe it will be a good change from avoiding church ... and those 'church people.' I guess I'll soon find out.

He decided to lay out his clothes for the day and get ready first and read the Press with any remaining time. As he shaved and showered, his mind was busy.

Julie would be pleased to see me going to church. She was such an encourager ... helped me focus. I sure do miss that woman! So far all my attempts to find another soul mate have turned out badly ... some worse than others.

Once he slipped on his dress slacks, a new sweater and shoes that tastefully complemented them, he returned to the bathroom mirror. Brushing the hair on both sides and the back of his rather ample bald area and shaping his goatee, he mused ...

People say I look young for my age. Are they being sincere or just trying to make me feel good? Maybe losing a few pounds off the middle wouldn't hurt. My skinny doctor would certainly be pleased. I'm not that bad of a catch, am I? Is vanity a sin? Oh, that's right, my paper is waiting.

He scanned the news, the obituaries and was reading a few of his favorite comics when Phil came up and quietly stood in front him. Looking up from his Lazy Boy, he immediately noticed that Phil was amused.

With a gleam in his eyes and smirk on his face, Phil chided "Brushing up on our current philosophy are we, Doc?"

"I just enjoy a little good light humor. But the comics do shed some very clear light on current values ... and no one can deny that Charles Schultz's cartoon, Peanuts, is some of the finest philosophy in modern times."

"Okay, point well taken. Are you ready to go?"

"Yes, I am!"

They slipped on their winter dress coats and headed for the garage to Pete's new dream machine.

As they pulled out of the driveway, Pete gave Phil a quizzical glance. "These friends you want me to meet ... They seem to be important to you. How did you meet them ... what's the connection?"

"They ARE important! Like family! They're in a small group I joined recently at Valleyview Church. You know where that is, don't you? "

"No, but I'm assuming it's on a hill someplace. These church people you hardly know them?"

"I guess you could say that; but I've come to trust them."

"Trust them?"

"Yes, with my problems ... loss of work ... need for a place to live. They were praying with me and suddenly you became the answers to our prayers. "

"I know that's what you said when I offered to let you live at my place – but do you actually believe that?"

"Yes, I do – don't you?" Phil challenged.

Slowing down to make the turn, Pete hesitated then said "I don't know quite what to believe these days, Phil."

"Well, we're here now so please hold your verdict until you've had a chance to meet my friends, deal?"

"Deal." Pete agreed.

At the door a younger couple greeted them with warm handshakes and toothy smiles. Pete had forgotten his gloves – so the warm hands were a timely welcome.

They seem nice enough ... are they for real? They're the greeters. It's their job to be nice.

Phil brought him back to the mission at hand when he said "Pete, I'd like you to meet the Stowycks."

Extending his right hand, Pete's mind was momentarily distracted.

Stoics? Seems appropriate.

"Uh ... hello."

Their demeanor and reception were considerably less enthusiastic than the couple at the door – even austere.

Weaned on pickle juice. Hmm, reminds me of a few of the old timers from my youth. Maybe they don't want strangers to break up their comfortable little group. Do I come across like that to my students?

Next he met the Gladdings.

They sound better already. Hmm ... they're upbeat ... kind of cordial ... even jovial. Now we're talking! They actually seem to be happy to be here. I like them! They even dress happy. Dress happy ... what's that?

The final introduction before finding their seats was the Kinnards. Pete tried his best to conceal his intrigue at their name.

Canards ... I certainly hope they don't live up to ... or down to its meaning. Church people are often accused of being phony and believing in MYTHS. That would certainly be a tough name to wear. Maybe they aren't familiar with the term. Some interesting people here.

Entering the auditorium, they discovered the only empty seats were near the front. Pete felt like every eye was watching him as he made his way to the second row. He estimated the room capacity to be about 150. There were very few unoccupied chairs.

This is the early service. I wouldn't want to be crowded in like this with a bunch of rowdy kids in the contemporary service. Does that make me a grumpy old man?

After an enthusiastic welcome and some announcements, the music minister led the choir in a song that Pete knew all too well ... It is Well with My Soul, Julie's favorite.

He closed his eyes, clenched his fists and tried not to show his lack of composure.

If this is some kind of joke, God ... if you are God – I don't find the humor in having to sing THAT song. Is this how you welcome me back? Don't be so sure I'm back ... I'm just here.

Most of the congregational songs were familiar to Pete and didn't provoke him like the choir's presentation. He sang like someone who had nothing to hide.

I wonder how many of these people are hypocrites just like me. I can do this.

The lead pastor, Josh, was a young fellow in his early thirties. A neatly groomed mustache appeared to be an attempt to hide his boyish face. It wasn't working for Pete. Once he stepped up to the podium and introduced his theme, he had Pete's undivided attention.

Okay, Preacher Man, what new insights can you share about the prodigal son that I haven't heard before? Give it your best shot – I'm listening.

He shifted in his chair, folded his arms across his chest and sat back confident ... ready – or so he thought.

Josh's opening statement was like an arrow to Pete's heart. "Somewhere in our crowd today is a person who is running from the Lord. Let me warn you ... you can't out run God! He knows who you are and where you are."

Did Phil tell him I would be here today? How else could he know? Was he guessing or playing the odds. Hmm ... do preachers gamble ... or have special insights?

Shifting artfully in his seat, he leaned forward with new interest – placing his forearms on his thighs. He was ill at ease but he certainly didn't want to show it.

Stay cool, Pete. Don't let this preacher corner you. What did I get myself into? This is not going so well. Maybe I should have stayed in bed.

After about thirty minutes of presenting his case like a veteran prosecuting attorney, he gave a most convincing closing statement.

"I'm sensing, that we may have a prodigal with us today who is under some serious conviction. Remember, my friend ... you can't run from God but you can run TO Him. It's your choice."

The music minister led the congregation in several verses of Just as I Am, encouraging anyone who had 'business to do with the Lord' to come forward. Shifting his weight from foot to foot and gripping the chair in front of him, Pete stayed put.

I'm just not ready for this right now ... too many things to resolve ... way too many.

~ Chapter Eighteen ~

After the church service Pete had the dubious pleasure of meeting some of Phil's other small group friends. They stood in the parking lot and chatted until they noticed that their parking spaces were needed by the younger set who were coming for the next service. Before they were able to escape, several of the young men came over to scope out Pete's new toy.

One of the more outspoken admirers asked "You driving this fine machine in the winter?"

"Oh, it's my winter car." Pete chuckled.

Phil shot him a disapproving glance and muttered under his breath "Yeah ... and your summer car too."

Once the crowd cleared out they hopped into the object of appreciation and cruised off to the delight of everyone but Phil.

"WHAT was that all about?" he asked.

"Just having a little fun with the kids. Is that so bad?"

"I thought it was rather immature. These are my church family! YOU don't have any right to treat them like that."

"LOOK ... I didn't ask to come to YOUR church! It was YOUR idea!" *rather sensitive aren't you, pal?*

After the brief but heated verbal exchange the short drive home was totally silent. Both men went to their neutral corners and didn't speak for most of the afternoon. Pete slipped off his shoes and reclined in his Lazy Boy.

After what seemed like just a few minutes, he felt something tapping on his toes. Peering through his extremely heavy eyelids, he saw Phil standing by the footrest of his recliner. He wasn't smiling.

"Hey, man, what's up?"

"We need to talk, Pete. I owe you an apology."

"Hey, it's no big deal. I know I was out of line back there and you had every right to call me out on it."

"Yes, you were ... but so was I for the way I unloaded on you. So, please accept my apology and forgive me."

"Only if you can accept mine and forgive me as well."

They agreed, decided to put it behind them and move on.

Somewhat hesitantly Pete asked "They mentioned the evening service in the announcements. Do you usually attend at night as well?"

"Most of the time, but I'm not legalistic about it. Why do you ask? Did you have something else in mind?"

"I just wondered. If you plan to go – that's fine but I think I'd like to stay home."

"If you want to talk about it ... I can stay home too."

"Are you sure? I don't want to make you backslide or anything like that."

"Missing one night hardly constitutes backsliding."

"No, but missing as much as I have certainly must."

"Why don't I stay here and we can have our own little service?"

"You're going to preach at me, are you?"

"Should I? Any suggestions about a text or topic?"

"No! I had quite enough for today already!"

"How so? Did the preacher hit a tender spot?"

"It did seem as though he knew I was going to be there. You didn't ..."

"Tell him? No! Besides he would have had to change his sermon at the last minute. That seldom works well."

"If you didn't say anything, that's even more alarming."

"Are you thinking what I'm thinking, Pete?"

"Okay, tell me ... has he been preaching from that text recently? This wasn't his typical 'expository' teaching, was it?"

"No and no. It was more of an evangelistic message."

"Or like a prosecuting attorney going after a powerless defendant in the courtroom!"

"Were you uneasy there, Pete?"

"In a word ... YES!" *More that I care to admit.*

"Why?"

"My life has been a mess lately, Phil. I know some of the things I've been doing ... places I've been going are not right. In fact they're dead wrong!"

"Do you want to talk about it now?"

"Not yet. But ... we do have some of my history to pick up on. Where did we leave off" *Please ...back to my story.*

"Let's see ... you started going to that Bible club to meet some elusive beautiful girl ... who suddenly ... and mysteriously disappeared."

"Oh, that's right. Well, I became a regular at the club and invited some of my friends and they seemed to have a good time ... behaving themselves ... and so did I."

"That had to be a real change for you, right?"

"Yes! I met some really amazing people and some sweet girls who were initially cautious about associating with me. My reputation had preceded me – unfortunately!"

"Did that change?"

"Well, I went to the Saturday night 'rallies' downtown and met some girls from other schools ... ones who didn't know me. I dated some of them first. Later, the girls from my school decided they could trust me too."

"So, you're in the tenth grade and dating?"

"We called it dating. I didn't have my own wheels, so we would meet at the rally and sit together and each go our separate ways afterwards. That was the extent of it."

"How did you get to and from?"

"Sometimes my parents would chauffer me. That was embarrassing! As often as I could, I would ride with an older friend. That was cool!"

"So, how did things go for you with this club?"

"Time seemed to fly by. Our club met at 7:50 on Friday mornings and I was there early most of the time. We did some fun things. It wasn't just Bible study. We did have quiz teams, so even the Bible study was exciting!"

"Quiz teams?"

"Oh yeah! Students would memorize entire chapters and books of the Bible to prepare for competitive quizzes."

"Were you on a quiz team?"

"Not yet. I had a major decision to make first."

"Decision?"

Yes. You may remember my earlier profession of faith. I never really developed any evidence that it was real. One Saturday night, at a rally, I went forward to make certain that I was truly saved. From then on, I was different."

"How so?"

"I gave my testimony in club and started to carry a small Bible on top of my books. I had it with me throughout the entire school day."

"How did that go over with your classmates?"

"Some mocked me and others were just curious. This gave me an opportunity to witness and invite them to our club. Many came. This got the attention of the other clubbers."

"Did they approve of your friends coming?"

"I'll say! They even elected me as club treasurer for the next school year. Quite a change from my penny pitching days in intermediate school back in Jackson."

"You mean 'penny pinching' don't you?"

"No, I mean 'pitching.' A bunch of us guys would pitch pennies to see whose penny ended closest to a certain line on the sidewalk. The winner got all the pennies."

"You were a gambler too? Don't get too pious, pal. Judas was the treasurer for Jesus and His twelve disciples."

"True – but being a traitor was the farthest thing from my mind. My new faith was my life!"

"Oh the joys of a fresh faith! Do you miss it, Pete?"

"Yes I do, Phil, and each day gets a little harder. It's a battle I must fight ... and hope to win."

"This battle ... when did it start?"

"Not for decades. But, for now can we stick to these more pleasant times?"

"Sure, Pete. Did you do anything besides the Bible club in high school?"

Oh yes, I had a part-time job working in a neighborhood grocery store in the ninth grade but quit for sports."

"Sports?"

Oh yeah, I went out for football in the ninth grade. I made the team but only got in on a handful of plays the whole season. I tried again the next season but got hurt and gave up on organized football for good. I played with a bunch of neighborhood guys and did alright."

"Any other sports?"

"I got four letters in track, played on the church basket-ball and softball teams. Something I enjoyed the most was the sandlot baseball games we had at Briggs Park. Some of the varsity players from area high schools would join us ... so we had some great games."

"Sounds like you had a lot going on. Did you have a summer job?"

"Not until after I graduated from high school. I just kept busy having fun and enjoying my youth. The summer flew by and, before we knew it, we were back in school."

"So, now you were Bible club treasurer. How did that work out?"

"I got more responsibility than I bargained for. The new president seldom showed up and the other two officers, both girls, didn't want to be in charge. So guess who?"

"You?"

"Yes me. I was thrust into leadership ... sort of a baptism by fire – if you will?"

"How did that work out?"

"Better than I expected. My first challenge was going to the principal's office to get permission to place posters in the hallways promoting the club's activities. He made some joke about missing me lately. All of my previous visits were for bad behavior."

"How did you respond to that?"

"Straight from the shoulder. I told him that my life had been changed by God and he wouldn't have to worry about any more detention visits from me."

"And he said?"

"He calmly signed my permission slip and said 'We'll see, son, we'll see.' and went back to his paperwork."

"Did he see?"

"Absolutely! AND every time I went to his office on business, he commented on how active our club was and the good influence we were having on his students. That came as a real encouragement to me – since I knew he was a member of the most liberal church in town."

"So, you haven't said any more about your dating life."

"You haven't asked."

Okay, I'm asking now."

“YFC – Youth for Christ, sponsor of the Saturday night rallies, also held monthly skating parties. I loved to skate. It was there I met one of the sweetest girls I’ve known.”

“Let me guess – Julie?”

“No. Remember I said we wouldn’t meet for several years yet? This gal was from a suburban high school on the far side of town. She was a year younger than me and. most importantly, the right height. Her parents were the nicest Christian people. They had six children and my sweetheart was the oldest. That meant she was called on to babysit often but I cherished any and all the time we could enjoy together.”

“I take it you were quite smitten by her.”

“That is an understatement for sure. I even rode my bike out to see her a couple times. It must have been at least 20 miles one way. Once, her mom felt sorry for me and drove me home because I stayed until almost dark. She even helped me put my bike in the back of their station wagon”

“So did this become a steady arrangement? How did you get to see each other?”

“Yes! Our parents would bring us each to the rallies and skating parties so we were able to see each other quite often. We ‘went steady’ until ...”

“Until what?”

“A couple of my buddies teased me about being tied down and dared me to break up. Neither of us had dated anyone else for eleven months. The first time I was able to drive my dad’s car; I drove out to her place and asked her for my class ring. She gave it to me reluctantly and I drove back home. A few hours later I realized what a stupid mistake I had made. I was too proud to admit it.

The next time I saw one of her sisters, I learned she was dating a young fellow from her church. A few years later they were married. They are still happily married today and I am happy for them. I was too young, foolish and proud to know what I was giving up."

"That must have been a hard lesson."

"Yes it was! I remember it to this day! But, I had to get over it because some very busy days were ahead for me."

"Busy days?"

"Yes, I was elected to be the official president of the club and shortly thereafter elected as president of the council overseeing 36 clubs in Western Michigan."

"Wow!"

"I'll say! All this ... for a shy little country boy."

"So this new responsibility ... what did it involve?"

"I was invited to speak at several clubs and share with them some of the things we were doing at Creston that caused our club to more than double in attendance in two short years. The speaking became something I learned to enjoy – especially with young people who were excited about their faith and wanted to share it with their friends. I also presided over our monthly regional meetings."

"Your club more than doubled?"

"Yes! We went from about 60 to 150. We set a record of 250 when we showed one of the YFC teen movies."

"That's amazing!"

"More importantly, during my senior year we had twelve first time decisions for salvation."

"What a blessing! How did you do it?"

"I didn't! We involved as many people in the program as possible. The club grew because kids CARED!"

"Did this create a stir in the school?"

"On the lighter side, my fellow athletes referred to it as my fan club. I was quick to let them know that it was Christ who the clubbers worshipped and NOT me."

"How about your principal? Did he come around?"

"Only to the extent that he liked the behavioral changes in kids who joined the club. It made his job easier. A couple Jewish parents complained to him about their sons claiming to have 'received Christ as Savior.' He told them if they wanted to start a Bar Mitzvah club to feel free to do so ... but this club was staying.

Unfortunately, just a few years later, Madelyn Murray O'Hare had all such clubs removed from public schools. It seems that many local administrations overreacted to the Supreme Court's interpretation of our Constitution concerning the relationship between church and state."

"I'm afraid you're right. That's quite the story, Pete. I understand why you wanted to continue talking about it."

"Yes, those were definitely the good old days."

"You know, my friend, there can be better days ahead."

It was late. They finished off Pete's leftover Christmas cookies and eggnog ... and called it a day.

~ Chapter Nineteen ~

Because the holidays occurred on the weekends, classes wouldn't resume until January tenth. This would give Pete another whole week to discuss his life issues with Phil. He slept in and enjoyed the leisurely pace he had experienced recently. Waking, he reflected ...

How much should I share? Have I already shared too much? Is he getting bored? Do I consider this 'couch time' or what?

Then it hit him as he was sitting in his robe and slippers.

What's for breakfast? Where's Phil?

There was no enticing aroma of sizzling hot bacon – no freshly brewed coffee ... nothing.

I guess I was spoiled yesterday ... ah yes, to get me to go to church. He's a crafty one alright. But ... he seems to really care about people. That's a good thing. He doesn't give the appearance of being a 'soul hunter' like some guys I've known ...

His thoughts were interrupted as Phil burst through the front door. He was bundled in his warmest winter coat, scarf and zipper boots. His cheeks were flushed rosy red and he was breathing deeply. A frigid gust followed him.

"It's a bit brisk out there – invigorating!"

"If you say so ... I like my nice warm house – uh condo."

As Phil struggled to close the door, the furnace kicked on. Pete, shivering from the sudden cold blast, quickly found the closest warm air register and huddled over it.

"Sorry, Doc, I didn't mean to freeze you out!"

"You certainly made a hot cup of coffee sound good."

"Okay, put yourself together and we can breakfast too."

Phil didn't have to say that twice. Pete was ready in record time. Without shaving or showering, he threw on his jeans and sweatshirt ... brushed through his hair with his fingers, put on his coat and headed for the garage.

"Let's go!"

Phil just stood staring at Pete and replied ..."Like that?"

"Sure! You're hungry aren't you? Besides ... IHOP doesn't have a dress code."

So, they went for breakfast. This time Pete looked like the hobo. Some of his colleagues and students were in the restaurant but they didn't acknowledge him.

Do I look that different that they don't recognize me ... or are they too embarrassed to speak to me? Maybe I should have taken the time to spiff up.

Pete shoveled down his food. He had to escape his plight.

I guess I didn't realize that I had developed such an image. So much for the casual life during school breaks. Do I look that bad?

Phil detected Pete's discomfort and ate quickly too. As they were walking to the car, Phil asked "Were you a bit uneasy back there?"

“More than just a bit. IHOP may not have a dress code but it appears that the GVSU crowd does ... at least for faculty. Did you sense that I was being shunned?”

“Sense ... NO! I saw you being shunned.”

“Don’t let me go out like that again – PLEASE! I know you tried to stop me and I was determined to go like this. Next time hogtie me if I’m being bullheaded.”

“Sounds like rodeo talk. Are you a fan?”

“Not exactly, but I do enjoy watching an occasional western movie.”

“I do too ... especially older ones. You know, played by John Wayne, Gary Cooper, Glenn Ford and Alan Ladd to name a few. Oh, yeah ... and Tom Mix, Gene Autry, Roy Rodgers, Andy Devine ... the list goes on.”

“Most of those were in black and white, but we didn’t mind. When I was younger, that’s all we knew. Movies and TV were in their infant stages. Today, all those scenes seem very unreal. Back then we didn’t notice.”

“As I was growing up, the industry started colorizing some of the older films. That brought them back to life.”

“Yeah, but I can still enjoy one of my favorites – even without the color.”

As they were pulling into the garage, Pete suggested that they rent some of the old westerns and have a movie night with pizza and pop. Phil agreed and that concluded the reminiscing ... about old movies that is.

Once in the comfort and safety of the condo, Pete relaxed and slipped off his boots and hit his recliner. Motioning to an overstuffed rocker, he said “Have a seat, Phil. Can we continue with MY story?”

"Sure. Let's see ... I think you were a senior at Creston High School when we left off."

"Yeah, that was a busy year for me. In addition to my involvement with YFC and sports, I became very active socially ... especially dating several different girls."

"A recovery tactic? I mean ... from your disappointment over the breakup?"

"Without a doubt. I was hurting and it was my own fault. I was wounded but too proud to admit it. So, I refused to become too attached to any one girl. Dating became a game. One of my friends and I had a contest to see how many different girls we could date. We even kept a list so we could keep track. We both had wheels now so the challenge was on."

"Did the girls you dated know about your game?"

"Oh no! That was our secret. Can you imagine how they would feel if they knew?"

"I'm guessing like just another notch on your rifles to recall the western lingo."

"Yeah! AND if they'd found out, we would have been sent to the hoosegow, or even worse the gallows don't you think, partner?"

"For sure, and I wouldn't have blamed them."

"Me either ... but I'm older and wiser now."

"So, now I'm curious, how many notches did you have?"

"More than you could fit on one gun."

"HOW MANY?"

"Are you ready for this?" *I bet you're not.*

"I don't know. Should I brace myself?"

"Probably." Pete replied with a boyish smirk.

"Okay, shoot – pun intended."

"Well, we continued the contest through college – Julie was number one oh five."

"Seriously? One hundred and five? Did she know that?"

"Of course not! But one day our boys were talking about how many girls they had dated and asked me. It just slipped out. When she heard, she wasn't' impressed. She simply smiled when I told her that she was my last – and best."

"Slick trick, Doc." Phil chided.

"I was sincere ... but the boys decided they could beat my record ... and they did. Years later, their wives learned about it and they had a similar reaction to Julie's."

"Okay, we're getting ahead of ourselves here. What about your friend? How did he fare in your contest?"

"He fell in love with a girl from the YFC club and, after serving time with Uncle Sam, got married. Although I won the contest, he never regretted losing. In fact ... he really considered himself to have won. She was far better for him than my hollow victory of numbers was for me."

"And, you were still single for a while then, right?"

Dropping his chin, Pete muttered "Yup, 'til I was almost 24 and out of college. I think I was still looking for someone like my crosstown sweetheart."

"So, you're in your senior year of high school. You seem to be quite busy. Were you a good student?"

"Not really. I aced the classes I enjoyed and the others ... well ... not so good. The problem is that I didn't enjoy enough classes."

Did you have a favorite?"

"I would have to say Bookkeeping. After taking Algebra and Geometry courses until they no longer made sense to me, I took Bookkeeping in my senior year."

"Why did you consider it your favorite class?"

With a renewed enthusiasm, Pete chirped "I excelled with numbers, so it was easy for me. I had the best grades in the whole school in that class. There were only two other boys in my class ... neither were that sharp."

"That must mean there were a lot of girls."

"Exactly... twenty-seven ... all sophomores! Among them were some of the cutest girls in the school. Since I had mastered the subject, my teacher had me tutor those who were struggling. Needless to say, I was very selective in the ones I helped – only girls and ... OF COURSE ... the cutest ones." Pete crowed.

"You had it all figured out, didn't you?"

"Oh yeah, I was good with figures too!" *Oh boy was I!*

"Okay, cool down old-timer! We don't want you to blow a gasket. I'm sure you made the best of that situation and added a few more notches as a result. Were there any other classes where you excelled?"

"Not really. I was just an average student. I never studied and graduated near the middle of my class of 278."

"You've mentioned college ... how ... where?"

"I wanted to go to Taylor University but it was too costly and I certainly couldn't qualify for any scholarships. So my dad offered to pay my first year's tuition if I would go to our local Bible Institute for at least one year. That was too good of a deal to turn down. So I accepted. The humiliating part was that they would only accept me as a probationary student because of my low GPA."

"So you were on the hot seat to perform, right?"

"And how! Then they decided to seek accreditation as a degree granting four year Bible College. That's when things really started to get tough. Their grading system was so difficult that transfer students who excelled in the local junior college had trouble getting passing grades there. In spite of the school's change, I decided to stay."

"How did you do?"

"For the first time in my life, I had to study. I spent many all-nighters studying ... only to fall asleep in classes. I had a few classes that I enjoyed and aced. That helped make up for Greek."

"You didn't like Greek?"

"I guess you could say Greek didn't like most of us. We started with 36 in the first semester and ended the fourth semester with only NINE."

"And you?" Phil prodded.

"I think I was number eight ... only because I aced the final exam, which was a literal translation of a text. If grammar had been included, I would have failed. Greek grammar was not my thing. My grades in philosophy, psychology and Bible classes raised my average GPA."

"Were you able to spend all your time on your studies?"

"No. I had to work part-time to save up for future year's tuitions. I was still living with my parents but needed to pay for my transportation and most of my meals since I ate out regularly."

"Did you have time for any social life ... dating?"

"Of course! I used to say that I was a student full-time, worked part-time, dated part-time and volunteered in my spare time. Oh, and I was still involved in sports."

"Sounds like a pressure cooker life."

"You could say that. But, I was able to cram a four year education into only five years. I got my degree with no debt ... of course, no honors either."

"You mentioned volunteering ... what was that?"

After high school, I stayed on with YFC and worked in their counseling room and coordinated their follow-up program for a couple years."

"And, you were just out of high school?"

"Yeah, I was nineteen or twenty."

"Quite a responsibility for your age, wasn't it?"

"I seemed to be thrust into some big jobs at early ages. It has a way of turning up the heat on that 'pressure cooker' you mentioned earlier. I would be called upon for more challenging things in the days ahead. I think I've bent your ears long enough for now though. Let's do lunch."

"You definitely have an interesting story, Pete, but we do have this whole week to explore it."

"You're a patient man, Phil; it shouldn't take that long."

~ Chapter Twenty ~

After lunch, still sitting at the table, Phil prodded Pete to continue his story. "Before our break, you mentioned that you would be called upon for more challenges. Are we ready to talk about them now?"

"Are you sure you're ready to hear more?"

"Hey, man, you listened to my story. Now it's my turn to hear yours."

"But ... mine's much longer. Let's sit in the den."

"So, you're much older, Pete ... no offense."

"None taken. But I do seem to be getting bogged down in a lot of details. Maybe we can edit some of the rest of the story before you fall asleep over there in that cozy chair."

"Only if you're up to it. I'm wide awake and my time is yours. Maybe we can call it bartering for my rent?"

"You don't owe me anything for lodging. I'm finding your company a balm for my grief. 'balm' ... how's that for a good biblical term?"

"I appreciate that and am always happy to help. I seem to recall something about a 'balm in Gilead' ... wherever that was. I guess I'll have to look it up."

"Do you mean 'Google it' or something like that?"

"Or ... look it up in one of my Bible reference books."

"That reminds me, I really admire your library."

"Last night you mentioned some rallies. What were these rallies? Did kids actually go to them? What did you do there?"

"When I first started going, they were held at the Ladies Literary Society ... hardly an appealing place for most of us guys to go. Only a hundred or so attended there. But they moved it to the Mel Trotter Auditorium and were able to accommodate SEVERAL hundred. They filled it to capacity every Saturday."

"How did they get so many kids to come on a date night? Wasn't there anything else going on in town?"

"We didn't just sit around reading the Bible and having snacks! We had special guests who appealed to youth like Christian comedians, Christian professional athletes, and Christian musicians. All of our guests were vitally interested in kids and were themselves in the prime of their lives. We had all the latest Gospel films including the best Billy Graham Series. Mind you these were not just preaching films. They included a brief message but were exciting life action stories. They were powerful!"

"You were able to get hundreds of teens to come every Saturday night ... that's impressive!"

"Absolutely, every Saturday during the school year. In fact we had a thing we called 'Youtharama.' It filled the 5000 seat Welch Civic Auditorium for several successive nights. It was great!"

"How, in the world, did you get so many kids to come?"

"We always had an attendance contest between all the area schools and gave special treats to the winners. For the winners at Youtharama the prizes were pizza parties. As usual, Creston won more than its share of contests."

"Not to change the subject, Pete, but you really have some great memories. You seem to find great pleasure in talking about them."

"Yeah, I guess so. But that's all they are ... MEMORIES. I can't find comfort living in the past. That was decades ago. I need to make peace with today."

"Are we moving in that direction?" Phil challenged.

"Slowly ... but are you beginning to see the history I'm dealing with?" Pete's voice quaked slightly.

"YES! It seems quite amazing to me."

"That ... that's a big part of the problem ... how far I've fallen from my glory days. I feel like I've hit bottom."

"Can't get any lower than that. Where to now?"

"If you don't mind, there are more blanks we have to fill in so my story makes sense to you."

"Okay, Pete, lead on."

"It's interesting that you say it that way. It seems like I have been thrust into leadership my entire adult life. The editors of my high school yearbook placed the saying 'Let Daniels do it' next to my senior picture ... I've been trying ever since to get it done."

Phil chuckled "Okay, so what's next?"

"Well, after two years in the counseling and follow up work at YFC, and based upon my being well known as the former area president, I was then elected as president of my denomination's hymn sing program."

"Oh ... what did that involve?"

"I worked with 24 area churches coordinating locations for the hymn sings and arranged the programs. The host church provided special music and their pastor usually gave a brief devotional talk. We provided our own song leader and I gave the announcements and handled the attendance contest. You might expect that the host church would win each month. That wasn't the case though. Each church's goal was based on a percentage of their membership. Often a the smaller church came with a big crowd and took home the plaque for the month."

"How long did you do that?"

"I served for two years ... until I finished college. It was near the end of my second year that I met Julie."

"Finally! How did you happen to meet her?"

"Well, you do recall I was dating several different girls at the time, right?"

"Yes, but what does that have to do with it?"

"She was there with Danny, her steady boyfriend. He and I had recently entered a bowling league as partners."

"So?"

"They had arrived late, just as I was finishing my part of the program, and were standing in the church foyer. I told Danny that I had a problem deciding where to sit because there were three girls there that I had dated in the previous week. One was in the balcony and two on the main floor."

"What did you do?"

"We both treated it as a big joke and I didn't take a seat."

"I guess you solved that rather easily, right?"

"Only temporarily."

"How so?"

"I learned later that Julie was not impressed – well not favorably anyway."

"Who told you?"

"Julie did. She went home from the hymn sing and told her mother all about this cocky guy. She said I was the most disgusting person she had ever met."

"Sounds to me like you didn't get off to a very good start with her. How did you recover?"

"Her Danny Boy made the mistake of two-timing her ... and with one of their co-workers no less. She gave him back his class ring and said they were done."

"So, then you moved in, right?"

"Not so fast there, pal. Remember I'm not exactly on her top ten list. In fact, I was one to be avoided at all cost."

"Well, you obviously won her over. What happened? What did you do to win her over?"

"One night, about a week after the break up and before bowling, Danny was bemoaning the fact that he had messed up. I told him if he didn't apologize and make up, I was going to ask her out."

"I'm guessing you followed through on your threat."

"I sure did! After another week, Danny was at my store and mentioned that it was her eighteenth birthday and he still hadn't made amends. It was February 27."

"I picked up my office phone and had him call her. She answered and he just stood there speechless. I grabbed the phone from him and wished her a happy birthday. When she asked who was calling, I simply told her it was

Danny's bowling partner. I mentioned that we had met at a recent hymn sing. She didn't need to be reminded ... "

"Then what happened? Did she hang up on you?"

"No ... but she became very silent. Then I did it! I asked her out ... for a date. She hesitated briefly and then said 'Sure, why not!' I'm not sure which surprised me the most – my asking or her answer. Our first date was on March fourth. It almost sounds like a military command, doesn't it?"

"So ... that was rather bold. What did your friend say?"

"He was shocked, but I think he was a bit relieved that he didn't have to eat humble pie. Her mother, on the other hand, that's a different story. When Julie told her about our upcoming date, she asked if I was the same disgusting guy. Julie replied that I was and let it go at that."

"You must have won her over quite quickly."

"Actually, I think I won her mother over first – then the rest of the family ... except her dad."

"Did he ever ...?"

"No, he died from a heart attack. They reassured me that it was not my fault. He had a long history of strokes and heart attacks. He died at 71. Back then that seemed old ... not so much anymore. I'm almost there myself."

"That was the end of your 'dating career' then, right?"

"Yes it was. We got married on December 26 that year."

"How old were the two of you then?"

"She was almost 19 and very mature. I was almost 24 and, in some ways, still a bit immature."

"We had our first child 18 months later. I almost lost her giving birth to David and was hesitant to have any more children – but she persuaded me that it would be fine. We had two more in the next four and a half years. She was right ... everything was fine"

"How long were you married before she died?"

"We celebrated our 44th anniversary less than a month before. Those were some truly amazing years ... growing together, raising a family, continuing my education, still working to support our family and serving on various church and school boards, seeing our kids grow up and get married and then all those wonderful grandkids. It's all far too much to cover in these brief sessions ... we can discuss those details over the next several weeks."

Where do we go from here, Pete?"

"I think we need to get to the heart of the matter ... um, well ... the matter of my heart ... my life since Julie's passing. This is where the whole story has been heading and now it's time to deal with it." Pete barely whispered.

"Let's see, she died almost two years ago this month, didn't she?"

"Y-yes, January 19." Pete groaned.

"And it was sudden – no prior warning, right?"

"Only ... only flu-like symptoms that day. We had no idea what was happening. She said she'd call her doctor if the nausea, aches and pains persisted. By bedtime she was feeling much better again. So we thought she was just battling the 24 hour flu."

"Am I remembering correctly that she died in her sleep?"

"Yes, and that's exactly the way she wanted to go ... when her time came. She had seen slow painful deaths by her mom and both of my parents. In fact, she was their main caregiver and it left a profound impression on her."

"It must have been a terrible shock for you though."

"IT WAS! I was in my office working. When I went back to the bedroom, I found her lying on the floor. I tried to wake her up but she was limp. I called 911 and they talked me through CPR until the E-unit arrived. The paramedics tried to revive her for several minutes and then gave up. Just like that ... she was gone."

What did you do while they were working on her?"

"I watched and I prayed harder than I had ever prayed before. When the coroner removed her body, I called my daughter in the south and my two sons here in town. The boys came right over and spent several hours with me ... until they were satisfied I was going to be okay. They left at about three in the morning."

"How did you do during the visitation and funeral?"

"Amazingly well. I felt God's grace! We had an uplifting celebration of Julie's life and I found myself comforting those who came to comfort me. The first several weeks, friends and family surrounded me with loving support. When the visits and calls subsided I really learned what true loneliness was. I ... WAS ... ALONE." *And I still am.*

Easing out of the overstuffed chair, Phil said "We appear to be getting into some really heavy stuff and it's getting late. Can we pick up here tomorrow?"

Exhausted, Pete replied "Let's sleep in and do just that."

~ Chapter Twenty-One ~

After Phil retired to his domain last night, Pete dozed through the late news. He was alert enough to catch a Channel 8 storm warning for the next few days. Strong winds coming from the Dakotas were expected to bring several inches of lake effect snow to Western Michigan. The threat of heavy drifting and hazardous driving were likely. So when he got up, he wasted no time getting ready for the day.

With that forecast, Phil and I need to restock our pantries in case we're snowbound. We need to be prepared.

He called down to Phil and asked if he had seen the weather report. He had not; so Pete delivered the news and shared his plan. They decided to grab a quick breakfast at McDonald's drive thru and eat on the way to the nearby Family Fare.

As they were finishing their McMuffins in the parking lot, Phil asked "So, Pete, how bad is this forecast?"

"Bad enough to stock up on the essentials ... just to be safe, of course."

Neither of them gave any thought of the appearance of two men grocery shopping together ... that is until they entered the store. Several of the mothers seemed to give them suspicious glares and gathered their kids closer to their sides. The men each grabbed a shopping cart and started at opposite ends of the store – only meeting once in an aisle unoccupied by other shoppers. Pete was able to slip Phil several twenty dollar bills so they could maintain their charade at the checkout lanes.

Hmm ... the local news of campus diversity must be creating a cautious attitude in the surrounding area.. We know that we are just friends ... but this extremely conservative Dutch community seems to be on edge.

Once they had loaded supplies sufficient for an army, they headed home. Pete broke the silence.

“Can you believe what we just experienced back there?”

“These are strange days, Pete, and everyone has their guard up. We will need to be certain that our living in the same condo doesn’t send people the wrong signals.”

“How do you suggest we do that?”

“We could invite students over for pizzas and let them see our living arrangements. It wouldn’t hurt for them to get to know us better.”

“But ... we can’t invite all of them. There are thousands!”

“No ... but we could select a few of the more influential ones. Tank and Tiny ... some of the team. I’ve even given some thought to starting an off campus Bible study.”

“Here?” Pete objected.

“Why not? It’s the perfect place ... plenty of room.”

Hmm ... Tank and Tiny. I wonder if they’ve had any bites on the trap Wysocki set up for them to monitor. I’ll have to check with my sons.

“Can we discuss that further once we finish my story?”

“Sure, Pete, first we have all these groceries to unload.”

Noticing some dark clouds approaching from the west, they quickly carried their carload of groceries inside. Pete put his perishables in the fridge and frozen items in the freezer. Everything else was neatly arranged on shelves in his massive pantry. Phil lugged his stuff downstairs and did likewise. His pantry was somewhat smaller – just right for snacks. They ate most of their meals upstairs, or in restaurants, so that worked out just fine. Once he was finished, Pete called down to see if Phil wanted to come up and have a snack.

Maybe we can get back to my story.

Reaching the top step, Phil was loaded down with a bag of chips, two kinds of dip and several bags of cookies. He grinned and asked "Got any pop?"

"Just about any kind you can think of!"

"So, is this a guessing game?"

"Nope. Just want you to know ... I'm prepared."

"I've never doubted that, doc."

They sat at the kitchen table and munched on their snacks until Pete decided it was time to move to the den.

"You can bring the food with you. Let's get comfortable for our next session. Is it alright to resume?"

"Absolutely! Let's go."

Pete started slowly ... deliberately. "We – we were just getting to the point where my grief issues were ramping up ...where I was alone."

"I know this was a really tough time for you, Pete. We can take it at whatever pace you choose. No hurry."

"I need to fill you in on some background information so you will understand my story from here."

"Background?"

"Yes. When Julie and I moved into this community, we became involved in the association's activities. I was elected as president and she pitched in right alongside me. It soon became obvious to us, as our older residents left us for nursing homes – or their final destinations, that we needed to prepare for our final days. We discussed what the survivor should do when one of us died."

"That sounds pretty sobering ... even morbid."

"Not really. Death is a fact of life and being prepared is the best way to live the life we have. I strongly advocate end of life discussions."

"What did you decide?"

"Since I was five years older and Julie was in better health, I told her that the many widows here would give her many friends when I was gone. But, if she wanted to remarry, she had my blessing."

"How did she take that?"

"She questioned my thinking that I would go first, laughed, and joked about not wanting to marry another old man. Then she shot back 'YOU, on the other hand, will need a wife to take care of you and YOU have MY blessing.' She was right." *Was she ever!*

"Wow! That must have freed your mind about the idea of remarrying, right?"

"It freed my mind alright ... It didn't ease the search."

"Search? You didn't start looking right away, did you?"

"Oh, no! I waited about four months before venturing out. As I was grieving, I was starting to think of some of my friends who had lost their husbands and wondering if they were experiencing the same loneliness I was."

"What did you learn?"

"Not much ... I wasn't able to make contact with the few that I considered to be good matches. I did have a few casual lunches with a couple lady friends who had been divorced. These were just times to chat with no intention of making a romantic connection."

"How did that go for you?"

"I heard some real horror stories and my heart softened to situations that would have previously brought out a judgmental spirit. I had always taken a very legalistic view about divorce ... especially divorce and remarriage. As I look back now, I see those visits as life changing."

"Did you see any of them as possible spouses?"

"No, but it did open my eyes to broader possibilities. Not all of my friends and associations agreed with my views and that would create the need to make some changes for me."

"Changes?"

"Yes, I was on the advisory board for a mission agency whose policy was against any member in any capacity being married to a divorcee. Although I disagreed with their policy, I respectfully submitted my resignation. I was dating a divorced lady at the time and didn't want it to become a problem if our relationship became serious."

"Did it?"

"No, but I'm getting ahead of myself here."

"No problem, Pete, like I said earlier, you set the pace."

"I'm not sure if I mentioned how my son set me up on Facebook shortly after Julie's funeral. He told me that it would give me something to do during my lonely times."

"Facebook has certainly become a phenomenal success in the social media field. Did it help?"

"Oh yeah! I spent hours on it evenings and weekends. It's there that I met the first ladies that sparked an interest in my dreary life. Actually, I should say re-met them."

"Re-met?"

"Yes. The first one I found on my college alumni page. She was a gal I had dated a couple times way back then."

"The second one?"

"We'll have to get to her in a little while. Now, the first one I asked to be a friend and she readily accepted. We chatted, messaged, emailed and even talked on the phone several times before I asked if I could come to visit her. She lived on the other side of the state ... about 175 miles each way. She agreed and I went for her birthday and stayed in a nearby motel so we could spend a couple days together."

"Since you mentioned a second one, I'm guessing you didn't hit it off too well."

"We had a nice time but the spark just wasn't there. This was only four months since Julie's passing, so I called her on my cell phone as I was driving back and told her I was not ready to start anything serious."

"Is it time for the second one now?"

"Yes, I found her in early June. She was an attractive blond also from my almamater. She looked familiar, but because it was a small school, I knew we weren't there at the same time. I asked her to accept my 'friend request' and she agreed ... even though we weren't sure we knew each other. After several Facebook chats and a few phone calls, we agreed to meet.

She told me she would be going to the city's big annual festival with a singles group from her church. I had planned to go too ... on the same night – alone. So ... we decided to meet at eight o'clock at a certain location. I went early and enjoyed some of the ethnic delights only found at these food tents. Walking through the several streets of merriment, I became agonizingly aware of how really alone I was. I saw families, groups of teens and couples holding hands enjoying each other's company. I can still remember how alone I felt ... no friends ... no family ... no one to hold my hand ... ALONE!"

"That had to be painful, Pete."

"It certainly was. At eight o'clock we met at the designated tent. I had spilled chocolate ice cream on my shirt. When I spotted the attractive little blond, I was utterly humiliated and hesitant to meet her."

"What did you say?"

"I asked her if she could tell me how to get a chocolate stain out of my shirt? Her reply was 'If you can tell me how to get an orange chalk stain out of mine?' She must have brushed against some graffiti. We had a good laugh, the ice was broken and we were both relieved."

"That was better than either of you could have planned. Sounds like the beginning of a friendship ... am I right?"

Pete nodded "That describes it well. We dated weekly for nearly four months. We didn't realize it at first, but soon discovered our paths had crossed several times over the years. Our children even knew each other."

"That's amazing Pete ...several times?"

"The first time was at summer camp where I was athletic director for the junior high week. Mind you, I was only eighteen at the time and she was much younger ... and a camper. I didn't mention that I had never even noticed her but; she chuckled and told me that she remembered having a 'crush' on me."

"That didn't hurt matters now did it?"

"Well, the fact that I couldn't remember her didn't help but it was a connection. Then we discovered that we had worked at the same company after college. She was in the corporate office and I was a regional supervisor out in California. We had even met on one of my trips back to GR. We were, obviously, both much younger at the time ... and married."

"And ... you didn't recognize each other from that?"

"Keep in mind, Phil; over forty years had passed, and we had both changed over those years. But ... another ten to twelve years later our kids went to school together and her son and my daughter were in the same class together. With all those scenarios ... It seemed like destiny!"

"One day, early on, we encountered a couple who knew our families. After a brief chat with them, we turned to each other and both said 'We better tell our kids before they hear it second hand.' She had been divorced for a number of years – and her ex had remarried – so her sons were happy for their mom. My family seemed to accept the situation as well. It was later that I learned my sons just weren't ready to see their dad dating. I certainly was. My daughter showed support at every turn – and there were many turns ahead."

"It sounds like things were going very well ... for a while though."

"Yes. We enjoyed the entire summer together. She was a fine Christian lady highly principled and a lot of fun! I had strong feelings for her and couldn't hide it. Each time I told her how much I cared for her; she tensed up and told me that she suspected I was just transferring my love for Julie to her. When I pressed her for some kind of commitment and she didn't give me the answer I wanted, I would back off and suggest we stop seeing each other. To this she would reply 'Are you bailing on me?' It seems this conversation would come up every three to four weeks."

"Did you feel like you were on a roller coaster?"

"I sure did! I know I was definitely still hurting from the loss of my Julie but I sincerely believed we were meant to be together – as husband and wife."

"Wow, Pete, it sounds like you were in a bit of a hurry."

"You are so right ... and I see that now. My persistence and impatience in seeking some kind of commitment from her was the main thing that ended our relationship. We had some good times ... some bad times. We parted ways in late September and not on the friendliest terms. She was a delightful person ... but it just didn't work."

"So, Pete, that's two down ... were there more?"

"Yes. After four months seeing the same lady, I decided to be more casual in my dating. I needed time to recover from my first serious relationship since losing Julie. This helped me to avoid rushing to the altar."

"I signed up with two different internet Christian dating sites and studied the profiles of available ladies in my area. After eliminating most of them, I contacted the one I found most attractive. We met for pizza at one of my favorite joints. The hostess seated us next to a table of noisy and rude characters. Conversation was difficult – but the food was great. Walking to her car, I apologized and asked if I could see her again in a few days at a place where we could have a better conversation. She said 'No thanks, I don't think I'm interested.' It caught me totally off guard. So, I went back to the dating sites."

"Did you find some new prospects?"

"I did! I also reconnected with a gal from my high school days. These were all brief relationships and didn't bring my soul mate. They all were dead end streets."

"What did you do next? How long was it since Julie's death?"

"It had been about a year by then. The direction my path took from there is a whole story in itself. Let's take a break and pick up at this point later."

"That sounds like a plan, Pete. Hey! Did you see what's happening outside?"

The whistling wind was creating snow drifts throughout the back yard and the entire nearby golf course, tees, fairways and greens all blended together in a solid sheet of white. Michigan winters are beautiful if you can enjoy the scenery from the warmth of home. Pete and Phil were prepared and that was their plan.

~ Chapter Twenty-Two ~

Once Phil had left the room, Pete eased back in his Lazy Boy. He still seemed to be experiencing unusual fatigue. He had read about this being one of the many results of grief in a booklet from the funeral home. But it gave no information on how long it might last. All it indicated was that each person grieves differently and there was no set behavioral pattern to expect. Some items mentioned troubled him but he tried to put them out of his mind. He soon drifted off to sleep and strange dreams danced through his head ...

"Julie, have you seen my car keys? I need to get there NOW. They need me!"

"Who needs you, doc?"

"What ... huh ... oh, Phil. I – I guess was dozing. Did I say something funny?"

"You were calling out to Julie about someone who was in urgent need of your help."

"Oh, that's a dream I've had so many times lately ... and have no idea what it means."

"Dreams don't always need a meaning. Sometimes they are just random thoughts hooking up in our subconscious mind. You see, when we sleep, our conscious mind – the one that organizes and interprets our thoughts is at rest."

"I should have known my shrink friend would have an answer."

"Okay, doc, I'm not a shrink yet. I'm just repeating something I learned in one of my post grad courses."

"Well ... it makes good sense to me. Thanks!"

"Now that we have solved that burning question, I have one of my own."

"If it's about philosophy, I might be able to help you."

"Not exactly ... it's about spirituality. YOURS! Where were you spiritually during those days after Julie died?"

"Well, early on I was strong. The beginning of January – shortly before Julie parted this earth, we had started a daily Bible reading program. You know, one of those through the Bible in a year plans?"

"Yes! That's a good program."

"I was right on schedule the day she died and continued much of the year. That, along with staying close to my support sources ... family, Christian friends and church kept me on track. Most of that first year I was fine."

"You say 'most.' What happened?"

"I got lazy ... careless. It wasn't easy going to church alone when most of the other men were with wives."

"Did you drop out?"

"Those sound like rather harsh words ... but sort of."

"Sort of ... how do you sort of drop out?"

"It mostly started after my break up with the lady who had, unintentionally, won my heart."

"How so, doc? You're not blaming her, are you?"

"Oh NO! I take full responsibility. It's just that ..."

"That what?"

"She was a great influence for me and when she was gone it was easy to sleep in on Sunday mornings and do other things on Sunday evenings and Wednesdays."

"You were even going on Wednesdays?"

"That's right. Our pastor taught a class that was really stimulating. I went whenever I was in town."

"Dropping out – if I may call it that – didn't help, did it?"

"Not at all! It was the start of my decline ... backsliding."

"The start?"

"Yes, Phil, the start ... I did things and went places that I would rather not talk about ... not now anyway."

"That's okay, Pete, I won't pry. I respect your privacy."

"Thanks. I've already discovered that."

"So, this drop out ... was it complete?"

"It might just as well have been."

"What do you mean? What are you saying here?"

"When I went to church, I was cynical ... skeptical ... even critical. I was angry toward God ... and everything He represented. First He took my wife, my lover and friend for over forty-four years. Now he wouldn't let me find another soul mate. What kind of God would do that to a man who had served him all his life? After fighting Him, I finally wrote Him off just like He did me."

"Just like that? Was it that easy?"

"I didn't really have a choice. I wasn't about to be one of those hypocrites. It did take some time to feel normal."

"So you think it's normal to reject God?"

"It certainly seems to be here on campus. You can't deny that, can you?"

"I'm not here to defend the university but I do stand up for my God and EVERYTHING He does. He doesn't make mistakes, Pete, and He is absolutely perfect in ALL His ways."

"I wish I could believe that, Phil."

"You can – you MUST. We seem to have gotten off the story. There's still a year we haven't discussed."

"Are you sure you want to be talking like this to someone who is mad at your God? A heathen!"

"You're using heathen and backslider interchangeably ... they're not the same. You may be mad at God but I don't consider you to be a heathen. You're just confused ... floundering ... even flailing. We can still talk, Pete, but please be careful what you say about God. You do know He's listening, right?"

"I guess it's possible. Okay ... back to the story."

"Right, let's see, you had several dates that were not all that satisfying. Did you change your strategy?"

"Well, as you know, I was very active on Facebook and a couple singles dating sites."

"Yes?"

"One day I saw a Facebook post by the gal I had gone to visit several months ago ... the one from across the state. She wrote that she had lost a considerable amount of weight and had gained a whole new confidence."

"So did you ask for pictures?"

"Come on, Phil, I'm not that crude. I offered to help her purchase some new clothes."

"Did she accept your offer?"

"Yes, hesitantly and with some stipulations."

"Stipulations?"

"Yes ... she would select them, from thrift stores, and all in good taste ... nothing too revealing or sexy."

"Did you agree to her terms?"

"I agreed ... with my own conditions."

"What were your conditions?"

"Only two ... one, I got to come for another visit ... two, she would model her new wardrobe for me. She agreed."

"So, how long did you stay this time and how did it go?"

"Three days and it was FAN-TAS-TIC! I found a nice motel quite close to her place so we could spend all day together and return to separate places to sleep."

"You say 'fantastic' am I reading something into that."

"Okay, I'll have to admit to what some might call a male ego thing. Last time there was no spark. This time there were flames. She looked like an entirely different person. To me she was beautiful!"

"The change was that dramatic?"

"How do I say this? It wasn't just physical ... her whole demeanor changed. She was happy, confident, cheerful – even a little giddy. I think I fell in love right there."

"Just like that?"

"Something I learned from the Bible that I still accept is the fourfold nature of humanity. I think it was about how Jesus matured as a child. You know, mental, physical, social and spiritual. I believe a relationship is strongest when all four are in sync. Does that make sense to you?"

"Some of the best psychology is found in the Bible, so it makes perfect sense. It sounds like things were turning around for you ... you're still single. What happened?"

"I spent every weekend that I didn't have to MC our coffees with her. The trips weren't cheap with high fuel costs and motel bills – but they were worth it. Within three months we were engaged with a wedding date set for July 23."

"That sounds very promising. What went wrong?"

"She was living in the lower level of a friend's condo much like this one. Since it was fully furnished, she had most of her worldly goods stored in a rental stall near her place. To save on the monthly rent, I borrowed a friend's 24 foot truck and brought everything here. We spent an entire Saturday sorting out junk and deciding where to put the rest. That was near the end of June."

"Now most of her belongings were here. Then what?"

"We were scheduled to have our final premarital counseling session the next morning, during the Sunday school hour. She stayed with a neighbor lady down the street. "

"You say 'were'... do I see bad news coming?"

"Yes, in that it wasn't what I wanted to happen and no, in that was best it happened before a wedding.

"So what happened?"

Pete flashed a goofy grin "Isn't it about bed time?"

"Come on, doc, you can't leave me hanging like this!"

"I wouldn't think of it. So, just before I was supposed to pick her up to go to church, she came knocking at my door still in her bathrobe, hair undone and no makeup. She was crying her eyes out and, obviously, had not slept all night. I invited her in and asked what was wrong."

"Okay, doc, keep talking. You have my attention."

"She blurted out 'I can't go through with this. You're too good for me.' I was shocked and asked what gave her that idea? She didn't answer me and just handed me her diamond ring. I tried to reason with her. I told her I loved her and should know if she was good enough for me."

"What did she say?"

"Nothing. So I suggested she get some sleep and we could talk more at about 3:30 or 4:00. It was nine at that time. She agreed and I went to church and told my pastor about the change in our plans. He, calmly, reassured me and suggested that we postpone the wedding until a later date. I told him that was my plan."

"So, how did the afternoon conversation go?"

"It didn't. I called my neighbor at about five and learned my intended was sleeping. My neighbor asked if she should try to wake her up and I said 'no. just have her call me when she is awake.' I got her call at about nine. She told me her son and daughter-in-law would be at my place by ten Monday morning. They had to drive through the night from Mississippi – in a pickup truck with two kids, a twelve year old and a baby. They rented a truck just like I had borrowed and were at my place at eleven. They were not at all happy with the situation."

"I would think not! What happened then?"

"My golf league was on Monday evenings. I called her from the course parking lot to make certain they had made it home safely. She assured me that they had but showed no signs of reconsidering her decision. Although I wanted to, I didn't debate the decision. Her mind was made up and she wasn't about to change it. "

"Did you have any further contact with her?"

"I sent her a Facebook message telling her how sorry I was that it didn't work out. She sent me a response that implied that it was entirely my fault and that she 'loved me but wasn't in love with me' ... whatever that means. She certainly didn't act that way when we were together. I know her first marriage was a disaster. That could have been weighing heavily on her mind. Anyway, she is a wonderful person and I wish her all the best. "

"That's quite some story, doc ... stranger than fiction. I'm sure this didn't help you in your spiritual battle."

"It was like gasoline on flames, Phil ... gasoline on flames!" *No it didn't help in the least."*

~ Chapter Twenty-Three ~

After a restless night reliving the events of their latest conversation, Pete finally dozed off in the wee hours of the morning and woke up later than usual. He could hear Phil rummaging around downstairs in his new library. Throwing on his robe, he called out.

"What's going on down there?"

"Sorry ... did I wake you up? I was just looking for one of my old textbooks."

"No, I just got up a few minutes ago and wondered what the ruckus was in the lower realms."

"Is that what you're going to call my living area? Why not just call it the Cave of Abaddon?"

"That's pretty harsh, Phil, I was referring to location ... not description. Besides, I'm the one who is straying from the fold."

"You do know there's a cure for that, right?"

"I'm working on it but the path seems to be over strewn with many obstacles."

"Why don't we each shave, shower and make ourselves more presentable and we can discuss it over brunch?"

"Okay, but I'm not sure we'll be seeing anyone else today. Have you looked outside? It's nasty out there!"

"True, Pete, but I'm sure we'll both feel better."

They decided to reconvene in about an hour at Pete's kitchen table for coffee and toaster pastries – not exactly the breakfast of champions ... but both men felt more like average guys today.

Pouring a cup of fresh hot coffee and carefully removing a cinnamon Pop Tart from the toaster, Phil expressed his concern about last night's conversation. It wasn't so much what they talked about as much as what they had skirted over.

"Pete, we talked in detail about your life before and after your years with Julie ... but very little about your time with her. Is there something you are avoiding or trying to hide? Why so little about those forty plus years?"

"As I mentioned before, in the future we will spend days talking about those wonderful years. There are thousands of precious memories that we could talk about 'til our dying days. The more I think about them the harder it is for me to deal with the loss ... the hurt."

"I'm not trying to make it difficult for you, Pete."

"I know. Let's just leave it at this ... our marriage wasn't perfect – but it was pretty darn close. We each had a few growing pains but we learned from them. One thing we learned very early in our relationship was that WE were a team! Anything we encountered ... we encountered as ONE! It was us for or against all others. When our kids came along they discovered they couldn't get us to take different sides with them. They either had OUR approval or they didn't – period. You have no idea how much trouble we avoided by our united front. If we disagreed, we did it in private and in a most civil manner. Some of the incidents that seemed traumatic back then – were merely speed bumps as I look back at them now."

"Is that all you want to say about those years?"

"Well I should add that we did enjoy our kids and they made us proud in many ways. They were now all happily married and had given us eight wonderful grandkids by the time Julie passed away. One more has been born since."

"I can see that it must be hard for you to look back at those times without hurting deeply."

"More than you may ever know, Phil. The more I think about it AND my recent rejection by a lady I had hoped to marry the more I wonder."

"Wonder what?"

"Where ... WHERE is YOUR GOD when I need him?"

"He's YOUR GOD too, Pete!"

"I wish I could believe that!"

"You can, Pete ... YOU MUST!"

"I'm not even certain there is a God anymore and if there is why I have been dealt the hand I'm holding."

"I can understand how you may feel that the deck is stacked against you. Pete, but life's not a game of cards or a crap shoot. Life is serious business and you need to be careful what you say about The Almighty!"

"He hasn't been very mighty on my behalf."

"Let's talk about this, Pete. You seem to be very angry and confused. This is a long ways from where you were not that long ago."

"I know ... how the mighty have fallen."

"You were NEVER mighty, Pete. At your best, you were

totally dependent on the Grace of God. If you thought of yourself as 'mighty,' you were already on the wrong track. I'm sure you didn't mean what you said."

"No, I guess not, but things were once so different."

"What changed?"

"Life ... plans ... religion ... purpose ... you name it."

Refilling his coffee cup, Phil asked "Do you want to talk about it? Where do we start?"

Sighing deeply, Pete sat quietly running his finger around the rim of his cup ... then said "religion I guess."

"Okay ... what about it?"

"When my faith faltered ... if it was faith ... anyway when I started to have my serious doubts, I went to different churches hoping to find answers."

"Why didn't you simply talk to your pastor?"

"Too embarrassed! I was considered a model Christian. How would that look to all my piers?"

"Couldn't you have scheduled a private session?"

"I already had the failed engagement and had cancelled a premarital counseling session. How would it look then to go as an upstanding church member who was angry with God? No, when I went to church – infrequently – I went where I could go unnoticed. At least that was my plan."

"Did it work or did people recognize you?"

"For the most part, I was able to slip in and out alright. But the more places I visited the more disappointing my visits became."

"How so, Pete?"

"Some of the churches I attended were like big business. They processed their visitors like they were a shipping department ... got your name, slapped a label on you and moved you to a certain section of the auditorium. Others ignored you completely – I actually preferred them so I could remain anonymous. But it would have been nice to see at least one friendly smile. They were stone cold!"

"Did you miss your home church?"

"Certainly, but it just wasn't the same being alone. The widows usually sat together but the widowers weren't so inclined. It was awkward sitting with married friends and felt strange sitting alone. Somehow, it was different in a church where I was a stranger."

"What about some of the other churches you visited?"

"Some were stiff ... formal ... too much like a monastery. Others were too showy with those new 'praise teams' and immodestly dressed and heavily made up women dancing around on the stage. They reminded me of circus clowns. Definitely not my cup of tea!"

"Hey, your cup is empty. Can I get you a refill?"

Shifting in his chair, Pete accepted the offer.

"Thanks, Phil; I hope I'm not boring you here."

"Not in the least! I'm finding your vivid descriptions most fascinating. How was the preaching at these churches?"

"It was every bit as varied as the rest of the services. As you know from an earlier conversation, I prefer to be taught and to make my own life application."

"Yes, and what did you find?"

"Real teaching seems to be a lost art in many churches."

"Really ... and what has taken its place?"

"Storytelling, reminiscing and video clips with a very brief personal app ... kind of a take-off on the new smart phones. I even saw skits with acrobatics – you know with gymnastic tumblers performing on stage. Again, I felt like I was in a circus."

"It sounds like you've seen it all."

"I don't know. But, I think, I was bothered the most by the preacher who strutted around the platform, shouting out threats of judgment and slamming his Bible on the pulpit. Babies were crying, elderly ladies sobbing in their hankies and others frantically wringing their hands. It wasn't a pretty sight. I couldn't wait to get out of there."

"So, did you go back to your own church?"

"No. I started to look elsewhere."

"Elsewhere ... where?"

"Other religions. Ones you would call cults or isms."

Standing – obviously not amused, Phil glared cautiously at Pete and blurted "cults ... isms?"

"Yes, Phil, I was desperate."

"What did you learn?"

"Everywhere I went, I found people who were blindly following belief systems that were totally foreign to my upbringing. Their leaders were all dead and their rules were most oppressive. Most of them offered no hope for a happy afterlife. Some worshipped gods who were just like them – hedonistic, sex-crazed and basically evil."

“Wow!”

“You say ’wow.’ Does it surprise you that ... I could, so easily, dismiss the world’s great religions ... as being unworthy of my acceptance?”

“No, Pete, I’ve studied them and reject them as well. But it does surprise me that you used the same Christian faith, which you claimed to have rejected, as the perfect standard by which you judged them. That seems a bit odd to me ... inconsistent.”

“I’m not sure that I rejected it. I was just having trouble making it work in my life.”

“Were you trying, Pete ... seriously?”

“Probably not.”

“I didn’t think so. You have heard the saying that one religion is just as good as another. That they all lead to God by slightly different paths ... all you have to do is be sincere, right?”

“Yes, I have but that’s just bogus. I learned that sincerity wasn’t good enough way back in early grade school.”

“That’s pretty early. How did you learn it?”

“I sincerely believed Grand Rapids was the capitol of Michigan. My teacher informed me that sincerity was good, but Lansing was the only acceptable answer.”

“That sounds like a very valuable lesson.”

“I guess it was ... I still remember it today. You know, as I think back about that ‘all religions thing’ ... they can’t all be right.”

“Okay, Pete, let’s hear your logic on this. I’m sure it will be airtight coming from a philosophy prof.”

"From the Bible we read that Jesus claimed to be God and demonstrated it by his works. Most popular religions recognize Him as a great teacher and wonderful role model – but not God. He can't be both. If He is not who He claimed to be, then He is a liar and a deceiver of the worst kind! Furthermore, He said He was the only way."

"You're a very good apologist for a backslider, skeptic and apostate, Pete."

"Thanks, I read a lot and try to have an open mind to good logic."

"That's very admirable! You seem to have a very high opinion of Jesus. Where does that come from?"

"Past experience and my reading. Even some of the most outspoken atheist and agnostics have difficulty rejecting some of the boldest claims by and about Him."

"Are 'atheist and agnostics' our next topic for discussion here, Pete?"

"I think so, Phil, but let's save it for another day. I have some reading to do and I'm guessing you do too ... that is, if you found the book you were looking for earlier."

"Sounds like a plan. Oh, by the way, what are we doing for supper? I don't think we want to venture out on the roads today."

Standing and stretching Pete replied "Not with my new toy in all that white stuff. Let's just heat up one of those pizzas we got for just such an occasion."

After polishing off a deluxe pizza, they decided to each catch up on some of their pleasure reading. The break was a welcome change of pace for Pete. He decided Phil probably was in need of a break as well.

~ Chapter Twenty-Four ~

A full week had passed since Tank and Tiny had taken the notice to the Lanthorn office. The well placed ad had been clearly visible in the campus paper since Monday. Their post on Facebook had been up for seven days. They reposted a similar request every day... to no avail.

With football season over and the ugly winter storm upon them, they were holed up in their apartment devouring pizzas, microwave meals, chips and guzzling Cokes. Their weight wouldn't be a problem until spring drills and summer two-a-days. The tiring wait for their keenly anticipated CALL was rapidly wearing on their patience. So far, all they had received was ridicule and scoffing from fellow athletes.

Slouching in his overstuffed chair, and bursting at the seams himself, Tiny bemoaned their plight: "We haven't even heard from the little red-haired girl from class. I was sure she would call wanting to help ... even for free."

"There you go again ... back in yer Charlie Brown mode. What is it wid you an' redheads?"

"It's not all redheads. It's THIS one! She's real purdy and seems ta be real sweet!"

"How do you know? You haven't even talked to'er."

"I said seems, dint I?"

"You haven't even gotten close enough ta know what she seems like. You're jus' dreamin' – that's all."

"Gimme time ..."

"You've had the whole first term. How much more da ya need? Some guy might just come along and sweep'er off her feet while you're draggin' yers."

"If he does, I'll knock'im offin 'is feet!"

"I'm sure that'll impress yer little redhead."

Struggling to lean forward and escape the clutches of his chair, Tiny was ready to refocus the conversation. "Ya think we'll ever hear from da thief, Tank?"

"I think so ... da plan should work. Even though finals'er over, mosta the football team got an extension on when we have ta take the exam. If the thief is on campus they should know that."

"Ya mean another Grand Valley student?"

"Who else would be able ta do it? It really seems like it'd be someone who could be on campus unnoticed."

They dropped the conversation and became otherwise occupied. Tank started searching the weather reports on his cell phone and Tiny decided to scan the recent posts on Facebook. Neither found anything to raise their hopes. With most of the faculty, staff and student body still on winter break, the campus Facebook page was very quiet. The weather forecasts were downright gloomy as well.

Suddenly, Tank's phone shrieked out its familiar shrill ringtone. Deeply engrossed in the weather app, he nearly dropped the phone in shock. Regaining his composure, he answered the call: "This is Tank."

The voice from the other end of the line was somewhat muffled – like a half whisper. “Yeah, Tank, dis is Chig. I’m callin’ bout your ad in da campus classfieds. Do ya still need help with your studies? Ain’t da finals over already?”

“Chig – huh ... where’d you get a name like that? You aren’t a student here, are you?”

“Listen, big shot, I dint call to answer a bunch a questions. Da ya still need help or not? If not, were done here and I’ll hang up.”

‘NO WAIT! Don’t hang up! I still need help but how you gonna help me? Ya certainly don’t soun’ like a tutor.”

“If ya want help, ya need ta trus’ me. Ya know what I mean?”

“And – why should I trust you. I don’t even know ya and I’m guessin’ ‘Chig’ isn’t even yer real name, right?”

“It’s nickname my boys put on me.”

“Your boys? You don’t sound old enough to be a dad.”

“I’m not ... I’m talkin’ about the guys in my gang – uh group.”

“So, Chig, how can you help me? Have you even taken any college courses? You sound like a young punk.”

Okay, Mr. college boy, maybe I ain’t never been to college yet. If that’s important to you, I guess we don’t have no business here.”

“Wait ... how are you gonna help me?”

“Well ... let’s jus’ say I got ta answers to yer big test.”

“The answers? Where – how ... did you get’em?”

“Dat’s none of yer business. I got’em ‘n you need’em.”

“Okay ... what’s yer deal?”

“I kin sell’em to you for two hunnert bucks ... ‘n no questions.”

“I kin only afford a hundred ... no more.”

“Don’t be stupid, Tank, a hunnert from you and da same from yer roomie and Walla! Ya gotcher two hunnert.”

"I don't think Tiny has that much to spare."

"He do or it's no deal, pal. It's yer choice."

He seems to be convinced we are interested in working with him ... why quibble over a measly hundred dollars. He's not gonna be getting any money anyway. "Okay, two hundred dollars. I'll scrape it up somehow. Where kin we meet to make our exchange?"

"Ya make it soun' like yer returnin' some clothes dat don't fit. Dis is a sale of goods ta you fer cash ta me. Pure 'n simple."

"Back to my question – where do we meet?"

"I'll call ya back in a couple hours. I gotta check on a few tings first. Just remember ... come alone 'n no tricks."

"Okay, Chig, you've got a deal. I'll be waitin' fer your call. I'd really like to get dis done as soon as possible."

As soon as they completed the call, Tank looked up Dr. Wysocki's residence phone and called him with the good news. Wysocki, professor and sleuth, was thrilled to hear that his plan was actually starting to work.

"Thanks, Tank, I've been waiting for this call. I have security on high alert. Where are you supposed to meet the perp?"

"He said he'd call me back in a couple hours with his instructions. I'll let you know as soon as I hear."

"You don't think he's setting up his own guard around the rendezvous location, do you?"

"I didn't think about that, sir. You're good at this."

"My family has a history of studying crime and criminal minds, Tank. I guess it's in my genes ... it's become a part who I am ... like a second nature."

"I'm certainly impressed by how your plan has worked so far. You seem to have thought this whole thing through, sir."

"I must admit that I've been very proactive in trying to get Mr. Simms off the hook on the theft of my stuff. I see an extremely bright future for him and want to do my part to see that it happens."

"I'm sure you will, sir. I better free up my phone so I can answer right away when the little weasel calls back. By the way, he calls himself 'Chig.' Pretty strange, wouldn't you say?"

"Yes, I would ... not nearly as impressive as Tank."

"Touché, Doctor Wysocki, touché!"

"Merely jesting, son, I'll be waiting for your call."

Chig's return call came earlier than he promised, making Tank wonder if Chig suspected anything fishy.

"Hey, Chig, what'sa plan?"

"Have dey plowed the roads on campus? The main roads is clear in Allendale. I'll be ridin' my bike if dey's okay dere. "

"Dey should be okay, Chig, dey have dere own plows on campus and keep tings in pretty good shape."

"Good, den I'll meet ya next to da tennis courts at four o'clock. Bring cash ... all in twennies ... and no funny business or da deals off. Unnerstand?"

"Yeah, Chig, I understand. I guess you'll prolly be da ony one out ridin' a bike in dis nasty weather."

"A man's gotta do what a man's gotta do. Iffin dere's more'n one, I'll be da one wid a backpack."

"Gotcha, Chig, see ya soon." *Wonder if he noticed I had picked up his slang? it just sort of slipped out.*

Tank immediately relayed the meeting time and place to Doctor Wysocki. He also cautioned him that Chig was wary and insisted that Tank come alone and no tricks. He then filled Tiny in on the details and asked him to stay by the phone in case of any problems.

"You gonna be okay wid dis, Tank?"

"He's just a kid ... I'll be fine."

"What if he's got a weapon?"

"If he does, he better be good wid it. Mr. Tank doesn't give second chances to bad guys!"

"I know. I've seen how ya hit da linemen on da field."

Tank bundled up in his warmest winter clothes and made his way toward the tennis courts. He was a few minutes early but wanted to scope out the situation. Everything had to be just right. Nothing could give Chig any hint that he was riding into a trap.

Hmm ... wonder if the campus security is here yet. If they are, they're doin' a great job of hidin'. This is their chance to shine. They can scoop the state and local police – right here – right now!

Checking his cell phone, he saw it was five 'til four. He also saw Chig rounding the last bend before the courts. As he hit his brakes, the bike slid on some ice and sent him flying. His backpack burst open spilling out watches, jewelry and other stolen goods. He had been a busy boy.

The campus police were on the scene in a flash, prepared for the worst. They surrounded Chig – weapons drawn.

"I – I don't think he's armed." Tank advised.

"We have to take every possible precaution." The lead officer replied. "You never know what to expect. Let's go kid. We can patch your wounds back at our station. Give him a hand, Hoekstra."

Hoekstra, a mountain of a man – bigger than Tank, reached down to assist Chig. The little guy kicked the hand that was trying to help him and spit out a string of curses that shocked even the tough lawmen.

Hoekstra responded "I see you like jewelry, kid. Get up and turn around with your hands behind your back. I have a nice shiny pair of bracelets for you."

Among the evidence the officers picked up, was a stack of papers. Tank edged over to take a closer look and, sure enough, there were the phony exam answers right on top.

After they had loaded him in a security car and driven off, Tank called Wysocki. "We have our man, sir. But he's just a kid ... just a kid ... can't be even sixteen yet!"

"Did he have the goods on him?"

"I'll say! Your exam answers and a whole lot of other stuff he must have stolen from other people."

"You say he's just a kid. Could he be part of a gang?"

"I think so. He mentioned 'his boys' and implied that he was in some sort of gang when we talked on the phone."

"What's happening to kids these days?"

"I don't know, Doc. you're the psychologist."

"Yes, I am, but even I struggle with our society today. Where is it headed? Things look rather bleak. "

"When you figure it out, please let me know. Do you think there's any hope for a kid like Chig?"

"There is always hope, Tank! If we lose hope – we've lost everything. The kid certainly does need help though ... someone to look up to ... to hold him accountable"

"I know that's what kept me from going bad ... that and football. Tough coaches probably saved my life."

"There you go, Tank, something to think about. I had better hang up now. I have a couple important calls to make."

"Yeah, something to think about ... uh who ... what are you saying, Doc?" But he was gone.

~

Wysocki first called David Daniels, asking him to relay the latest news to his father, who in turn could tell Phil. His next call went to Grand Valley administration. They needed to get the wheels of justice to get out of the ditch and start moving forward to clear his old friend Jimmy – who he now knew as Phil.

Phil, what a story! There is a man who has experienced some extremely hard knocks and has stood strong. I need to learn what keeps him going. He's like the Energizer Bunny. Well ... maybe just a very determined person. I will find out.

~ Chapter Twenty-Five ~

After a quiet evening and good night's sleep, Pete was ready to take on the day – inside anyway. There would be no venturing out on the roads for a few days.

I'm not taking any chances ... I know how to drive on bad roads but don't trust the other guy ... especially those young hot rods. They act as though they're invincible. Why they ...

Phil called out from below "Hey, Pete, you up already?"

Pete shouted back "Yup – and raring to go!"

Climbing the steps, Phil asked "Go where?"

"Actually ... nowhere, but I'm ready to tackle the day."

"I didn't think you wanted to drive in this weather."

"No, sir, but I'm ready for breakfast."

Now in Pete's foyer, Phil asked "What's it going to be?"

"How about some of the Bob Evans biscuits and sausage gravy we bought a bunch of the other day? I think they would hit the spot today ... and I must admit the spot needs to be hit. I'm hungry!"

"Me too, Pete, my place or yours – so to speak?"

"Let's do it up here. This microwave is bigger."

"Okay, I'll be back up in a few minutes. If you're ready before I get here, go ahead and start without me."

"So, you've learned not to deter a hungry man."

"Oh, yeah, back at my parents' dinner table ... as a kid."

“A worthy lesson for sure, Phil.”

Moments later, Phil returned and silence prevailed as both men concentrated on eating. As they were clearing the table, Phil suggested they start their discussion.

“I’m really eager to hear how you answer the claims of atheism and agnosticism – as a philosophy prof.”

“I do approach these issues more as a philosopher than as a scientist. We all have basic presuppositions. Mine have all been found in a strong commitment to a belief in God and the reliability of Scriptures. That has been the source of my dilemma recently. My doubts.”

“I can see how that would trouble you.”

“I think I’m starting to see light at the end of the tunnel.”

“That’s encouraging, Pete, can you explain that further?”

“Yes, but I think you’ll see as we discuss the subject at hand. As I just said, we all have basic presuppositions – beliefs. Atheists and agnostics have decided there is no God. In my opinion their decision is a matter of the WILL not a conclusion from serious intellectual study. If they are able to discredit the concept of a Creator – by accepting the claims of evolution – they free themselves from accountability. They can play by their own rules ... or no rules at all ... they think. We know differently. ”

“So then, are you saying that all atheist and agnostics are evolutionists? That’s quite an assertion.”

“I can’t say all of them because I don’t know all of them. The ones I do know are. It’s their easiest way out.”

“When did you start giving serious thought to your own personal philosophy, Pete?”

"It may surprise you, but as early as a simple country boy in the fifth grade. My best friend's dad had gone over the edge – flipped out – while in college studying science subjects that he could not reconcile. My friend and I liked to go fishing in a nearby creek ... a stream. His dad would always warn us about all the Pythons and Boa Constrictors. We knew better but to appease him, we told him we would be careful. This caused me to be leery of taking science too seriously."

"But, science is important, Pete."

"I'll grant you that, but science is ever changing. It has a very interesting history. Need a refill on your coffee?"

Nodding in response, Phil asked "How's that?"

"First let me tell you about an experience I had in the eighth grade. I was living in Jackson then and another friend – who incidentally died in high school from a drug overdose – was intrigued with evolution. He took me to this 'mad scientists' house to show me his fossils and artifacts. He was a self-proclaimed scientist and totally convinced evolutionist. When he spouted off on his well-rehearsed theories ... as facts, I simply asked him ... 'How did it all get started?' After some hesitation, he couldn't give me an intelligent answer. This question still stumps them today."

"What about Darwin's Origin of the Species?"

"Before Darwin, most science was based on the belief in an almighty God and an orderly universe. For over 150 years now, scientists have pointed to Darwin as the one who answered the big question ... we know he didn't. He merely observed mutations within a single species ... nothing more"

"I've heard a little bit about Darwin. Didn't he 'create' the Piltdown man in an attempt to prove his theories?'

"He sure did! There are some stories that he recanted of his views on his deathbed. Now, that's just a story I've heard. There's some strong scholarship that concludes he had no intention to have such an impact on history. But, even Hitler, Lenin and several other evil dictators have based their despotic ways on his teachings."

"Okay, so Darwin wasn't all the answer we were led to believe. What about the big bang theory?"

"Many scientist have shied away from it recently."

"Why's that, Pete?"

"Many reasons – what went bang ... where did it come from ... what made it go bang. Then there's the Laws of Biogenesis. If there was a big bang, the residual particles would have been permanently charred – not capable of forming or sustaining life."

"Interesting, but I must admit you're over my head now."

Pete went into a lengthy explanation and concluded "Don't feel bad – I'm learning some of this in my recent reading. But, I've always been bothered by the tricks the pseudo-scientists use to try to convince people."

Phil's interest seemed to be triggered "Tricks, Pete?"

"Yes, tricks! They ignore – or temporarily set aside – true laws of science in an attempt to prove theories such as evolution. Then they call unproven pet theories laws."

Now on the edge of his chair Phil says "What laws?"

"I already mentioned the laws of Biogenesis. Add to that the laws of Thermodynamics and, the most difficult for them, the laws of Cause and Effects. These are all laws that are universally accepted. There is no excuse for them taking such liberties."

"You're saying they violated these laws?"

"Their 'laws' of evolution are in direct contradiction to all of these laws. The second law of Thermodynamics states that things left to themselves move from order to chaos. They don't evolve ... they DECAY."

"And ... cause and effect simply states that every effect must have a cause, right?"

"That's it in a nutshell ... I couldn't have said it better myself. Then there is the scientific method. They totally modify it to suit their wishes. Mind you these are their laws not some radical religious notions."

"I'm not certain I remember the scientific method. Can you explain it to me?"

"I'll try. It goes something like this:

1. You ask a question
2. You do background research
3. You construct a hypothesis or theory
4. You test your theory by experimentation
   In other words, you attempt to disprove it
5. You analyze the results and draw a conclusion
6. You communicate your result

Okay does that make sense?"

"Yes, and I see the problem with the study of evolution!"

Excited by Phil's response, Pete says "Tell me!"

"They totally violate number four. They're not trying to disprove evolution. They have already declared it to be a law and are doing everything they can to persuade people that it's true ... especially innocent children, who revere and trust them. That's criminal!"

"I agree – it should be, but our public schools have bought into the error hook, line and sinker. The truth of the matter is that it is causing us to sink into mire worse than the slime from which we supposedly originated."

"So, you don't think that the universe is billions of years old?"

"No, Phil, that is just another way they explain things that they don't understand. I maintain that it takes more faith to believe in an atheistic evolution than to believe in an amazing Creator."

"Amen, Pete! Of course you know, one of the gurus in psychology had an extremely damaging effect on our views of the human ethic as well – Sigmund Freud!"

"Did you know he was profoundly influenced by Charles Darwin's teaching?" Pete asked.

"I've heard that before. It doesn't surprise me; they both deny any Supreme Being. Freud proclaimed that weak, fearful and desperate men created God to satisfy their longing for some long lost relative. I think he called it a 'grandfather' image. He saw the problem ... but didn't have the correct solution. Pascal, back in the seventeenth century, referred to a God-shaped vacuum in our inner being that could only be satisfied when God resided there. Saint Augustine said something similar."

"He not only has to be there, Phil, He also needs to be in control. That ... has been my struggle."

~ Chapter Twenty-Six ~

Their intense conversation after breakfast prompted Pete and Phil to take an extended break before continuing their discussion. They had agreed to restart about three o'clock – after having light lunches in their own places and spending a little alone time. Pete chose to read some more in a fascinating title he had recently purchased at his favorite bookstore. He shopped there regularly and was able to pick up several almost new conditioned books at a fraction of the list price. He had no idea what Phil was doing but was certain that he was enjoying the break as well.

A few minutes before three, Phil ventured upstairs to find Pete deeply engrossed in reading.

"What're you reading, Doc?"

"It's The Case for the Real Jesus, by Lee Strobel. He's the author of several 'Case for' titles."

"You know, I seem to remember a similar title of his that I read some years back – The Case for Christ."

"He mentions that one in here." Pete says, lifting the book for reference. "How was it?"

"I think almost every book that he has written has been on the Christian bestseller list. Some even made it to the New York Times list. I'm sure you were able to read about his background – a former atheist and married to an agnostic."

"Listen to what they say about him in the author bio. He has a 'Master of Studies in Law degree from Yale Law School, was Award winning legal editor of the Chicago Tribune, has four Gold Medallion winning titles and the Christian Book of the Year in 2005.' How can a reader not be impressed by all that? I know I certainly was ... and he writes in such a comfortable style. His journalism training has served him well."

"You should read The Case for Christ, Pete. It tells of his search for truth and spiritual journey. If I recall he saw a dramatic change in his wife after she accepted Christ and he decided to check Christianity out. Like several other famous writers, he intended to disprove it ... but, after a two year study, he became a believer as well."

"He alluded to having written that one in this book. He stated that in this book he was revisiting the same – and some recent – attacks on traditional views of Jesus. He wanted to see if they created any damaging effects on the reliability of Christianity. In my reading so far, he finds no new concerns ... in spite of many vicious attacks by antagonistic liberals. Most of the attempts are based on faulty interpretations ... or total ignorance of the Bible."

"When you finish it, I'd like to borrow it. I'll see if I can find my copy of his previous work and we can trade. Does it seem strange to you? This conversation seems to pick up where we left off earlier today. Now ... I'd like to hear your views on modern atheism. You know – in the last several years."

Leading Phil to the den, Pete said "It may not be all that coincidental. My reading selection has been significantly influenced by the matters we've been discussing. I've also been trying to shore up my own faith."

"I'm glad to hear you're working on that, Pete."

"Thanks! We can continue our talk ... but ... there's one matter I need to clear up first ... to reiterate."

Easing into his favorite chair, Phil replied "What's that?"

"When we started talking about the beginning – about the arguments for creation versus evolution – I implied that my position was philosophical based on my training in, and understanding of, the Bible."

"Okay?"

"I guess you could say it's more theological – based on God's revelation. Am I making any sense here?"

"Um ... I'm not sure – keep talking."

"Well ... I don't just think about the Bible as a history book ... a science book ... or even a philosophy book. I accept it as the very Word of God – even in my times of doubt. I just can't escape it. It just makes too much sense to my way of thinking. It's consistent and coherent to use philosophical terminology."

"Are you saying that you ascribe to the old slogan 'God said it ... I believe it ... that settles it,' Pete?"

"I know it sounds trite when you put it that way – but do we dare to doubt the Almighty?"

"Many do, Pete. Even you seem to vacillate."

"You're absolutely right, pal, and God calls them ... uh us fools. I find that discomforting."

"True, but I don't dare call them fools ... or you a fool."

"I'm not suggesting that – but they are not so kind to the theists. They ... uh we are considered blithering idiots."

"Where are we going with this line of thought, Pete?"

"Well, we talked about the scientific method, right?"

"Okay, how does that fit in here?"

"One of its key elements is observation."

"Oh! Now I think I see where this is leading!"

"You tell me, Phil."

"The only one there to actually observe was and is God!"

"Exactly, and he inspired Moses to record it in Genesis."

"What about those who don't believe in God and think the Bible is just a bunch of myths ... folklore ... or even fairy tales?"

"That's their misfortune. Maybe they don't recognize the actual immensity of our God."

"You mean like all of His omni's? Like omnipotence, omniscience, omnipresence and so on."

"YES! Too many people create their own god – much like Freud claims. Unfortunately the finite little brain we humans possess is incapable of comprehending the true God, let alone creating an adequate one. Recently ... I read somewhere, that even the brilliant Einstein used a very small fraction of his exceptional mental capacity. We humans are amazingly wired – but at our best, we're no match for God. Is it any wonder that He calls those who deny His existence fools?"

"We still haven't talked about modern day deniers of God, but what about those who to blend science and scripture and espouse theistic evolution?"

"If we accept a belief in God, why do we have to limit His capabilities? Is He God – or isn't He?"

"The ones I've read say that He could have just chosen to use evolution as His way of 'creating everything.' How do we answer that?"

"Very simple – He couldn't!"

"But we say He is capable of anything. How's that fit?"

"There have been many simpletons who have come up with riddles about what God can or can't do. That's not my line of reasoning here. God, by His own decree, can NOT violate His nature. He is Truth – so He can not lie or deceive. In His Bible He explains how He did it ... and it wasn't by evolution!"

"How do we know that, Pete? Couldn't God have started everything and then let it take its evolutionary course? Isn't there room for accepting a blend of both theology and science here? Isn't that like intellectual suicide?"

"In a word ... NO! If we accept that theory we have some major problems as Christians."

"What problems?" Phil prodded.

"God states in Genesis that when Adam and Eve sinned, the curse of death was brought upon earth for the first time. Before the fall everything 'was good' in God's own words. Evolution is offered as a slow process requiring millions or billions of years. That would have produced innumerable deaths of failed mutations. And ... are we to consider our first parents, Adam and Eve, to be just a mythological explanation for the advent of mankind?"

"How does all that matter, Pete?"

"Well, the whole Bible stands or falls on the first three chapters of Genesis ... no sin – no need for a Savior. The entire Bible is God's story of redemption – nothing less."

"I guess I've never thought of it like that."

"Many others have missed that vital information as well. Another question I would ask the theistic evolutionist is this. 'If God just cranked up the clock and let it go, why did He become so involved with the Hebrew people'? He gave them specific instructions – in the minutest details about how they should live life and worship Him. That doesn't sound like a God who would leave things to chance."

"Wow, Pete, you've been studying all this haven't you?"

"I certainly have, Phil! It's not just an academic matter. It's life and death ... yours, mine and everyone else's."

Before Phil had a chance to respond, Pete's phone rang and he excused himself – walking back into the kitchen.

"Really? Fantastic! How – who – where – wh..?"

The voice on the other end of the line said "Hold it – slow down, dad, just let me give you the basics."

Pete paced the floor with a renewed bounce to his step. He giggled like a teenage girl. Phil didn't need to be a detective to see that his friend was receiving some really exciting news.

"Thanks, son, I'm sure he will be thrilled to hear the news! I certainly am!"

Turning toward Phil and almost tripping over a kitchen chair, Pete proudly announced "They got him!"

"Hold it, Pete, who got whom?"

"You're a free man, pal, they caught the thief."

Phil lowered his head, mumbled a brief prayer, looked up and tearfully shouted "PRAISE THE LORD!"

~ Chapter Twenty-Seven ~

The lead officer waited until Tank had completed his call and asked him to ride back to the campus security office with him, saying only "I may need you to corroborate or correct some of our boy's statements."

Knowing he had no choice, Tank complied. He had never been in that part of the campus before. His little indiscretions were too minor to merit the involvement of security and he was not inclined to just make a casual visit. Once inside, he was invited to sit in the reception area until another officer led him back to the holding rooms.

"I'm officer Kidder, son." extending his right hand "I understand you're a witness. Is that correct?"

"Yes, sir, they call me Tank."

"You're on the football team, aren't you?"

"Yes, sir, I play fullback."

"I thought I recognized you. Congratulations on your award! I was hoping for a better team record this year."

"We all were, sir, but we had a lot of young players. Next year should be much better. We really started to come together as a team near the end of the season."

"That's good – I'm a big fan!"

Walking through the facility, Tank was impressed with the ultra-modern equipment and professional staff. Since Grand Valley State was like a city in itself, he considered it necessary. Knowing about all this behind the scenes protection gave him an increased feeling of security.

“You may watch the questioning through this one way window, Tank. The young fellow inside is not aware that he is being observed. Please listen carefully to what he says – we want to be certain he is telling the truth.”

“Yes, sir, I will.”

Tank could hear the detective ask “What’s your name, son?”

“I ain’t your son ... dey call me Chig.”

“We can do this the easy way or ...”

“Okay my name’s Bobby, satisfied?”

“Let’s get one thing straight right now, Bobby! You will show respect and get rid of that attitude or we’re going to have some problems here. How did you get to be called Chig?”

“S’long story.”

“Okay, just give me the short version.”

“At camp.”

“That’s short alright, how about a few more details?”

“I’ze at dis camp fer poor kids an I got deze bugs on me in da woods. Da camp nurse said dey was chiggers er sumtin like dat. All da bullies started ta call me Chig an it stuck. I like it better’n Bobby. Has a kinda gang sound.”

“Are you in a gang, Bobby?”

“I got m’boys – if dats what ya mean.”

“Your boys ... are they a gang, do they have a name?”

"Dey do – but I cain't tell nobody."

"That's okay for now. We have ways of finding out."

"Ya ain't gonna torture me is ya?"

"That's in the movies, kid, this is real life. No, we're not going to torture you. Now then, about this meeting you planned with that big fellow we saw when we apprehended you. What can you tell me about that?"

"Meetin'! I wasn't going to no meetin'... I'ze just out ridin m'bike, nuttin more!"

"He said you had something you wanted to sell him. Are you going to deny that?"

"What did'e say I'ze gonna sell'im?"

"You tell me kid. Was it some watches ... some jewelry or was it some test answers?"

"Okay so I had some test answers – so what?"

"Where did you get them?"

"I found'em! Is 'at a crime?"

"Where did you find them?"

"I don't member."

"You're lying to me, Bobby ... where?"

"Don' I git a lawyer or sumthin'?"

"I think we can settle this without one. Okay, Tank, come on in!"

As Tank entered the door, Bobby pulled back in his chair. "Ya ain't gonna sic him on me, is ya?"

"Relax, kid, we're just going to get his side of the story. Okay, Tank, what can you tell us about this case?"

“Well, sir, I think we need to have Doctor Wysocki join us in this conversation. He has some information that you will want to see and hear.”

“Can you call him?”

“Yeah ...uh ...yes, sir, He’s the one I was talking with right after your men hauled the kid off. Okay, here’s his number ... it’s ringing now. Yes, Doc, this is Tank. I’m at campus security and they want to talk with you too. Oh yeah, bring that sheet you showed Tiny ‘n me in your office. See you soon – we’re waiting.”

The short drive across campus only took the doctor a few minutes and he was right there – evidence in hand.”

After introductions were made around the table, Doctor Wysocki handed a single white sheet of paper with neatly typed test answers ... in bold Tempus Sans type.

“Interesting type face, sir, what prompted you to use it?”

“Tank told me that the boy had some papers in his back-pack. Did you find them?”

“Let me check with officer Hoekstra.” He opened the door slightly and called Hoekstra into the room. “We need to see the papers from the kid’s backpack. Please bring them in.”

Shuffling through several other meaningless pages they found it – a perfect match to the one Wysocki supplied ... typeface and all!

“What do you have to say for yourself, son?”

This time, a defeated Bobby didn’t object to being called ‘son.’ He was in desperate need of a friend – and he knew it. He put both hands on his forehead, rested his elbows on the table and said nothing.

"Okay, Bobby, we know you stole the professor's laptop. Do you still have it in your possession?"

"No ... I uh ...I sold it."

"If we can recover your computer, Doctor Wysocki, we'll have to notify your insurance company and get their instructions on how to proceed with your claim."

"They have already purchased a replacement for me."

"It sounds like your claim will stand uncontested then. It's not likely that we'll find it ... and if we did ... that it'd still be in the same condition as when you had it."

"I had everything saved onto a flash drive so all my data is preserved. Besides, I didn't have anything important on it – that's all on my desktop."

"Now then, Bobby, about the watches and jewelry – do you remember where you stole them?"

"I think so ... why?"

"We checked with the local and state police and you have no prior arrest record."

"Dat's true."

"With Doctor Wysocki's permission, we would like to give you a chance to clear yourself."

"Really ... how?"

"It won't be easy for you but we don't want to see a young fellow like you ruin your life for a few hundred dollars' worth of stuff."

"But ... I done stole it. What're you sayin'?"

"If you will return the goods to the people you stole them from – we'll call it good and wipe your record clean.

Tank, we need you to go along for moral support."

"Yes, sir" he smiled "I was just wondering if that would be possible. I'd really like to help the little guy."

"I ... I don' Unnerstand. Why ya doin' dis fer me?"

The officer in charge grinned and replied "I'm playing a hunch here, Bobby. I know I'm taking a risk – but ... as you might say it ... I'm 'BETTIN' ON YA.

One of the other security men let slip "While we've all been in here, we had people out there checking on your home life. You've had it pretty rough, Bobby, and we want to help. You see – cops have hearts too."

"Chee tanks, sir, I don' know what to say. Life's bin a mess an I jus' tryin' ta git by, know what I mean?"

Tank, the professor and the tough burly cops were all having a hard time with leaky eyes. Finally one of the officers spoke on behalf of the others "We really can't identify with your situation, Bobby, but we DO want to help you AND your family. We're not sure exactly how just yet ... but we'll figure it out."

Tank went around to Bobby's side of the table and asked him what he thought of how things turned out.

Visibly shaken, he trembled and choked out something about it not being what he expected. "Is dey fer real, Tank, dey serious? Dat's jus' too good ta be real!"

Tank couldn't answer. He just gave him a firm pat on the shoulder.

It was cold and late, so security gave Bobby a warm meal and cot to sleep on for the night. They called his home to let them know he was alright. There was no answer.

Tank arranged for a meeting with Bobby, was dismissed by security and headed back to his apartment – all the way wondering *how are we going to do this? Can the kid actually remember all the places he stole things? What have I gotten myself into, anyway? I guess it's like so many things ... time will tell.*

Back home, he filled Tiny in on the events of the night and really strange way everything ended. After listening intently, Tiny replied smugly "Looks like you got yerself a job there Bubba."

"Don't think you're off the hook here me, big guy!"

Still trying to recover from their shocking assignment, they sat quietly for a few minutes. Tank broke the silence "What's to eat?"

~

A few hours earlier, a short distance off campus, two older men were discussing their supper plans. Pete, still ecstatic from the good news phone call, suggested that it was time for Phil to celebrate his being found innocent and free to return to his job soon. "We need to do something special tonight! This is a big occasion, Phil. Let's find us a couple of big steaks and do this thing up right!"

"Sounds great to me! My treat ... uh ... that is if my credit is good with you."

Pete chuckled "If you insist, I'm sure you'll be getting a nice fat check of back pay. So, I think you're a safe risk."

Since the storms had subsided and the snowplows had done their usual excellent job, Pete felt safe to drive the Lexus. Allendale had a number of eateries – mostly fast food and short order places. This occasion called for one of those elegant places ... so McDonald's was ruled out. Phil said he had never been to Ruth's Chris and wanted to go there. "It may be my only chance so let's do it."

"You'll love it, Phil!"

"Have you been there?"

"Not this one, but I went to one in New York ... on my publisher's tab. My editor wanted to discuss a pending contract ... and I think he wanted to establish in my mind that I was still dealing with the right company."

"Did he convince you?"

"Ruth's Chris convinced me first. After a meal like that, I was in no condition to argue."

The normal half hour drive into the city took a bit longer and piqued their anticipation. Once seated, they were both thankful that they had taken the time to dress appropriately. This was the gathering place for the rich and famous. Neither of the new guests felt like they qualified as either rich or famous – but they enjoyed their meal and left the who's who crowd to flatter and cajole each other.

On the way home Pete said "You dropped quite a wad of cash back there, Phil."

"It was worth it, but it's probably the first and last time."

Pete laughed ... then became somber. *Julie and I never went there. She probably wouldn't have enjoyed it. She preferred the simple life. I miss her so ...*

~ Chapter Twenty-Eight ~

Pete spent the first couple hours Friday morning, in his sweats as usual, responding to his latest emails. Then he scrolled through the latest posts and checked for any messages on Facebook. He hadn't heard from Phil yet but assumed he was sleeping off last night's big feast. Shortly after ten his office phone rang. He answered "Good morning, this is Pete."

"Yeah, Pete, this is Wysocki from psychology. Jimmy ... uh ... Phil the former janitor, I hear he's staying at your place. Is that true?"

"Yes he is, Doc, but what do you mean by 'former'? My son just called last night to tell me you helped them catch the real thief. Now he can get his job back, right?"

"Not exactly, they had to hire someone else to fill the position. The maintenance work couldn't wait until he was off the hook – so to speak."

"W- wait a minute ... they can't just let him go like that. He is an innocent man! He is entitled to his job!"

"You're right, Pete, and that's why I'm calling. The top brass here is anxious to make things right with him. Can you and Phil meet me for lunch at the Grand Coney at about noon? We have a few things to discuss."

"We'll be there, Doc."

Pete alerted Phil of the unexpected meeting and quickly put himself together. They left with time to spare.

On the way, Pete informed Phil that his old job was no longer available but Wysocki seemed to have some kind of plan up his sleeve. “He told me that administration wants to make everything right with you. He said that he had met with them and shared his thoughts and they were very receptive. I think you would be wise to hear him out before reacting to losing the other job.”

“As my senior, Pete, you have been ... been like a father to me. I appreciate your advice ... and I agree.”

“It’s not that I’m all that wise – but I’ve dealt with these people for a number of years and they have always been more than fair.”

Pulling into the lot, they had to park quite a distance from the Coney door. Their host drove in right behind them. Because they were all a bit early, they were able to beat the noon rush and were seated immediately.

Pete introduced Phil to Wysocki and was surprised to learn that his fellow prof knew so much about his new house guest.

Wysocki started the conversation “I’ve heard some very impressive things about you, Phil. Is it alright if I call you by your first name – your real name? I feel kind of strange calling you Jimmy.”

“Please do, I just went by Jimmy because it fit my job. I understand someone else has been hired in my place?”

“Yes, Phil, what you were doing was too important to be left undone indefinitely. But please listen to my proposal before you make any hasty decisions. Let’s order first and we can talk more while we wait for our food. Order whatever you like – this one is on the university. They insisted and I didn’t argue.”

Neither of the two guests was very hungry and declined to mention their celebratory meal last night. Since they didn't have a breakfast, hot dogs seemed like a strange brunch. They each ordered the single dog special which included fries and a drink. Wysocki, on the other hand, loaded up. Pete had heard about his appetite. It wasn't exaggerated – by any means.

"Okay, fellows here are my thoughts. I'm told that Phil is very close to having his doctorate in psychology. I met this morning with the powers that be and shared my plan with them. They were as excited with it as I am. It would be an understatement to say they want to resolve this embarrassing predicament they are in. Being a state run institution, they must comply with some very stringent policies and procedures. That's why you were suspended, Phil. Now that the real thief has been found, they are ready to issue you all your back pay. You should be able to pick up that check early next week. That's not the best part ... but our food is here – let's eat."

"That check will help me catch up on some things I've had to let slip, sir." He quietly bowed his head and prayed a tearful word of thanks – and not just for the meal. Pete noticed Wysocki's furtive glance at Phil.

"You have a reputation for being a man of faith, Phil."

"Does that bother you, sir?"

"No" he said chomping down on one of his hot dogs. With his mouth half full, he continued, "Im fact is can be a positive factor im formin good character." He took a drink and swallowed. "As long as one doesn't become too fanatical about it and try to proselytize others."

"What would you call 'too fanatical'?"

"If you try to convert students or faculty and it interferes with your work, or you get preachy."

"Have you heard any such reports about me, sir?"

"No, I haven't and do you have to keep calling me 'sir'?"

"What would you like for me to call you, s – uh?"

"Call me Doc if you like but don't patronize me."

"I meant not offence, s – uh Doc."

"Okay, I know this is probably awkward for you so let's move on to the topic at hand – my plan."

"Yes, sir ... uh ... Doc."

"This is what I proposed to my superiors. They accepted it ... the entire package."

"Package, Doc?"

"Yes, Phil, Package."

"I've requested that the university allow me to take you on as my assistant for this next term. Then bring you on board as a teaching fellow beginning in the fall term this year. This comes with the appropriate scale salary, paid insurance and, if you so desire, on campus housing. At the same time, you can continue working on your PhD. How does that sound so far?"

"So far ... what else could there be? I'm flabbergasted!"

"I would like for you to consider taking my position once you have your PhD."

"But ... what will you do?"

"I'll be pursuing my dream, son, just pursing my dream."

"Dream ... what dream?"

"I would love to move to the downtown Pew campus and become the head of the criminal justice department – to follow my family tradition. I've made that desire known to the president and board and they are open to it."

Pete, who had been quiet as long as he could endure, said "Wow! This looks like a win – win situation, guys!"

"The new term starts on Monday. We can ease you in for the first few weeks then it's full steam ahead. Are you interested in coming aboard, Phil?"

"I'd be a fool not to be, Doc, yes I am!"

"I have a feeling that our students will accept you with open arms. I've seen how they treated you as a custodian. If that's any indication – and I think it is – you're going to have a great reception. Just don't blow it with your religion, Phil. You can live it just don't push it."

"That's always been my policy, Doc. If they can't see it – they won't hear it."

The meeting ended on a much higher note than it started.

~

On their way home, Pete and Phil were as giddy as a couple of little kids. Life was good and it was getting better. However, this news meant they only had a few more days to finish Pete's long saga.

"I guess we need to finish your story this weekend, Pete. It looks like we're both going to have our plates full come next week."

"I think we can do it. The end is in sight."

Pete rounded the last corner before coming to his place and hit the button to his overhead door. “I can remember when we had to get out in the cold to open our doors the hard way. This is so much better – until the power goes out. Then it’s back to the old way.”

“Your generation has given us many time and energy-saving gadgets, Pete – as long as we have power.”

“Without that power, we are lost.”

“My point exactly, Pete, we need the power.”

“Are you implying something more than I’m hearing?”

As the door closed behind them, Phil responded calmly “What do you think?”

“I think it’s an open and shut case and I’m not referring to the door. You’re trying to tell me something about my story, aren’t you?”

“Well, let’s talk about it more tonight over the last of our cider and donuts. For now, I need to collect my thoughts from our mind-blowing meeting with Doctor Wysocki.”

“Are you going to be hungry for supper?”

“I don’t think so. I’m trying to unknot my stomach and wrap my mind around the doc’s plan. He certainly has an amazing sense of direction. But, on the other hand, he doesn’t seem to have his life built on a firm foundation.”

“That could be said about me too, Phil.”

“No, Pete, your house is built on the Rock. You just seem to be operating with some of your circuits flipped off. Let’s pick up on this line of thought – say about six. That should give me time to unscramble my mind.”

~ Chapter Twenty-Nine ~

Pete was, once more, in uncomfortable territory – alone in his thoughts. *Did Phil really mean what I think he meant? Circuits flipped off? He was talking about loss of power ... we need to clarify this before discussing anything more. I think I know where he's going with this – but ...*

After considerable brooding on his latest conversation with Phil, he decided that he would meet the question head on.

I'll bring it up as soon as he hits the top of the stairs. I wonder if it has anything to do with Julie's death.. He seemed to imply that I had some sort of disconnect. Losing Julie was certainly a big loss of connection for me. We weren't expecting that we'd be separated so soon – we had plans – big plans – long-term plans. Now ... here I am with a boarder my son's age. He's someone to talk with ... but certainly doesn't fill the void. God knew what he was doing when he provided Eve for Adam. Why did He take Julie from me? I know, God, you took everything from Job and left him with his wife. But ... she wasn't the patient and gentle comfort that Julie was. Yeah ... Old Job thought he could hold You accountable, God. You sure told him! Now ... I feel like You're telling me.

Exhausted from his grief battle and from wrestling with One whom he could not defeat, Pete drifted into a deep sleep. His Lazy Boy cradled him like a baby and he slept until he was awakened by Phil.

"Hey, Doc, you were sawing logs like you had an entire forest to clear. You ready to finish your story?"

Pulling the lever forward and lowering the footrest he freed himself from the grip of his chair. "I think I need a strong cup of coffee first. Would you like some?"

"No thanks, I never drink the stuff after about noon."

What time is it now?" Pete asked stretching his arms, yawning deeply and rubbing sleep from his eyes.

"A little after six. How long have you been sleeping?"

"Not long enough." He filled a cup with water, heated it in the microwave and added a huge spoonful of instant coffee. "This bucket of mud should do the job. Before we finish my story, Phil, I want to ask you about the 'flipped off circuits' you talked about before our break."

"Ask away, Pete."

"Were you referring to my losing Julie as a flipped off circuit or disconnect?"

"Not exactly, you had no choice in that matter. What I was suggesting is the things you did to exacerbate your dilemma – your doubts."

"What things?"

"All of them were choices you mentioned having made as you described your journey through grief."

"Choices ... what choices?"

"I think I can illustrate. Do you have a Bible handy?"

Stepping into the den, Pete replied "I have several but I keep my favorite here on the mantle." Artfully, he wiped a thick layer of dust from its cover and handed the King James Bible to Phil.

"What's that in your other hand, Pete?"

"Dust, Phil. But what's your point? I already told you that I'd stopped reading it, didn't I?" *Here we go again ...*

"Yes, Pete, the dust merely confirms it. But, hear me out. I think it was the first, and most important, circuit that you flipped off. You stopped reading this Book. Whether it was a conscious decision or just something you let slip, the results were the same. Let's look at Psalm 119."

"I recall memorizing a couple verses in there as a grade-schooler. Could it have been nine and ten?"

"The whole chapter stresses the importance of God's Word in your life, Pete, but I'm guessing it was nine through eleven. Those three verses explain very simply where your problems of doubt and wandering got started. Earlier, you mentioned going places and doing things that brought shame."

Looking at the verses he had highlighted sometime in the past, he read silently verse eleven. He'd read it many times before. *'Thy Word have I hid in my heart that I might not sin against Thee'. That nails it!*

"So you're saying Phil, when I stopped reading my Bible AND became less regular in church attendance; I was flipping off the circuit of God's speaking into my life."

"When you can't hear from God, you start to question His existence. You doubt."

"I know that for a fact, Phil. Separation from loved ones brings grief. Separation from God brings every kind of doubt and oppressive feelings of loneliness ... especially when you walked closely with Him at one time."

"Your answer ... your only hope, Pete, is to cry out to God in sincere confession and ask Him for forgiveness.

We have that promise in First John one verse nine. Look at this."

> If we confess our sins, He is faithful and just to forgive us our sins and to cleanse us from all unrighteousness.

"You know, Phil, I learned that one as a kid too. It just seems too easy to be true. I know it in my mind but it's a bit more difficult to wrap my heart around."

"Do you doubt God?"

"The more I've studied about Him the more I believe in Him. Moving from belief to TRUST is the issue."

"So, do you just believe like the demons? You believe He created everything! Why don't you believe He can help with your puny little issues? Why?"

"Oh, I believe He can alright ... but I'm so unworthy."

"You know better than that, Pete! None of us are worthy. That's why Jesus came to earth, lived a perfect life, died in our place – as payment for our sins and rose from the dead to prove our debt was paid! You've received Him as Savior. NOW you need to trust Him as LORD! It's time for you to get right with Him and put your life back together again. Stop wallowing in your grief and get the victory, pal."

"You're right, Phil, I need to get back to singing Victory in Jesus like I did before I lost Julie."

"Don't forget Julie is fully alive in His presence. That's what our brief life on earth is all about – getting ready for lift off. This is simply dress rehearsal for the real thing. You said it earlier ... she's far better off than we are right now. Can't you just rejoice for her?"

"Once I get my life squared away with God, I'm sure that many of my troubles and doubts will be resolved."

"That's not a good motive, Pete, being in fellowship with God is not some wonder cure for all of life's ills. You need to remember, that losing Julie wasn't a punishment for you – it was a reward for her. You're still here and are expected to live for Him ... no matter what trials come your way. You will always have His grace to keep you going. You just need to trust Him."

Pete downed his third cup of coffee. "That's a lot to think about. I'll need some time."

"The longer you delay – the longer you live in misery."

"I know, Phil, I'm almost there. Let's finish my story."

"Proceed at your own risk."

"That sounds like a scare tactic." *He just won't stop.*

"It's your life, Pete."

"Okay, you were asking about modern day atheists and agnostics. I'd say the atheists have become considerably more antagonistic and aggressive in recent years. Instead of just being passive, some very prominent writers of their persuasion have referred to themselves as 'Brights' and by inference theists as 'dims' or 'dulls.' They've purchased banners on the sides of city buses to propagate vicious assaults on Christianity. It appears that they want to decimate people's faith in an all-out warfare.

"Wouldn't they be better served by just ignoring religion altogether and wait for it to die from lack of interest?"

"They've tried that for years and it didn't work. They consider religion a threat to society and are even moving from reclusive 'Free Thought' groups to forming their own mega 'churches' to give their people a warm fuzzy feeling about NOT believing in a god or supreme being. It's actually become another religion. They want people to believe that atheism is now a mainline worldview."

"Is it?"

"Documenting actual statistics is not an easy task – but they do appear to be growing in numbers. I'm convinced that the intimidation tactics and authoritarian attitudes of pseudo-scientists have enticed many of our youth to buy into their deceptive theories."

"That's just it, Pete, aren't they pushing their theories off as laws – without any substantiating evidence?"

"Precisely, but there is another philosophical genre, that in my opinion, is also very damning ... and I use that term in the biblical sense. This group probably accounts for the largest part of the world's population."

"That's quite a bold claim ... do they have a name?"

"They're not an organized group but you find them in many cultures and social groups. The term that has been coined to describe them is 'Apethists.' They are totally absorbed in their worldly pursuits and are apathetical to any philosophical or religious involvement. A sad thing is that many nominal Christians fall into this category."

"Sounds dangerous, Pete!"
"You know some very stern biblical warnings, right?"

"Yes and one of them actually mentions neglect – which is exactly what they're doing. Some people think that if they don't decide, they can just get by on good works. It's like they think God grades on the curve and they're just as good as the next guy."

"They are in for a rude awakening!"

"True, Pete, but did you know, that in the Old Testament, God refers to 'watchmen on the walls'? He cautions the watchmen to be awake, alert and to warn those inside the walls of any impending attack. If they do so and are still unheeded, they are guiltless. But, if they fail to warn, the blood of all slain will be on their hands."

"Are you saying we are the watchmen?"

"In principle ... I think so. That is, indeed, also scary!"

"How do you think that works? The Christian message is so unpopular today. Christians are hated and ridiculed for their dogmatism ... an absolute God ... only one way."

"Our responsibility is to lovingly share the good news. The Holy Spirit does the convicting. Doing it, determines our rewards – not our entrance into heaven."

"Makes sense to me ... and this leads into our talk about agnostics. They're my favorite group to interact with ... somewhat of a contradiction ... almost an oxymoron."

"Did you do this often? I mean interact ... uh debate?"

"Often when I've mentioned my belief in creation ... and a Creator, they would say they were agnostics and could not accept the idea of any absolute authority or power."

"How do you respond to that argument?"

"I ask them if they are real agnostics."

"Why would you ask that?"

"They will usually respond in the affirmative. I then ask if they know the word's definition and its word origin."

"Which is ...?"

"It comes from the Greek word 'gnosis' which is the noun commonly translated 'knowledge.' When you add an alpha (the Greek 'a') as a prefix, it negates the word. So agnostic literally means ... no knowledge. They apply it to mean no absolute knowledge – or truth."

"So ... what's your point, doc?"

"When they say that absolute knowledge is impossible, they are making an absolute statement that contradicts their core argument. So, at best, they are skeptics."

"Agnostic ... skeptic – what's the difference? They're still unbelievers, right?"

"Yes, but as skeptics they leave room for a friendly and intelligent conversation. They seem to be more open to considering new ideas ... thus somewhat receptive to the gospel – when presented sincerely ... and lovingly."

"Makes sense to me, doc – as opposed to beating them over the head with the Bible. In fact, the Good Book gives clear instructions about our attitude in witnessing."

"Yes it does, Phil. By-the-way, I will be out for a few hours tomorrow morning ... just to let you know."

"Big date, Pete?"

"Not exactly ... it's a funeral. I don't think you knew him. He's a former pastor. We served together on the school board."

Duty calls ...

~ Chapter Thirty ~

Tank's souped up hot rod roared into the back drive of an old abandoned bar on the shady side of a nearby town. There were no trash dumpsters but there was enough rubble strewn along the back wall to easily fill one. A rusty fire escape hung precariously above the solitary door. Cardboard replaced a broken window pane and the hinges appeared to be nearing their final swing. He hadn't seen such squalor since last year on his team's mercy trip to the inner city of Detroit – where they gave Christmas gifts to underprivileged kids. Just as he was about to knock, Chig gently opened the door, holding tightly to the handle with both hands to delay its demise. Tank took special notice.

He seems to be aware of his miserable conditions and is trying to protect what little he has. At the security office he was protective of his family's plight. Oh good, he has his backpack. Here we go ...

"Hey, Tank, thanks fer helpin' me wid dis job."

"Yer welcome, pal, ja eat yet?"

"I had some cereal bout n'hour go."

"That gonna hold ya?"

"Til lunch ... how longs dis gonna take?"

"You tell me ... where are we headed?"

"Mos' of da places is nearby."

"Ya figgered out whatcher gonna say yet?"

"I thought chu were gonna help me."

Tank just realized *I'm becoming a mentor and need to use my best grammar*.

"I am ... but you need to come up with an apology that the folks are gonna accept. It needs to be sincere, short and sweet. You may want to take your time to say the words right. Don't slur ... know what I mean? "

"I'll try ... but what chu mean sweet?"

"Not cocky ... you know. Be nice. You are at THEIR mercy now. The stuff you stole ... it's not damaged is it?"

"It's all in da same condition as when I took it."

"Okay, let me hear what you're gonna say."

"I ... uh ... I'm sorry I took yer stuff and wanna return it. I din hurt it ... I hope ya kin forgive me."

"That's great, pal, and if they ask your name ... tell'em Bobby. I know you don't like that name ... but, trust me. You will find'em more forgiving to a Bobby than a Chig and you won't hafta explain it to everyone."

"Okay, Tank, I'll be Bobby fer now ... jus' fer now."

"We can discuss that later ... and we better work on your grammar later. I have some ideas for you."

"Which gramma ... you goin' ta da door wid me, Tank?"

"No! I'll let you off a couple doors away and you can walk to the door alone. Trust me. It's better that way."

"It seems like I'm havin' ta trus' you a lot."

"Yeah, you'll find it's a good idea to trust Mister Tank."

"I'm getting nervous, kin we start doin dis b'fer I tink 'bout it too much an chicken out."

"Be brave, little buddy, you can do this."

I may be able to help this little guy. He needs to be guided by someone he can look up to. Hmm ... now I'm sounding like Doc Wysocki. Yeah ... now I see what he was sayin. This was his plan as soon as he saw Bobby's troubled life. He's one sharp guy.

Tank watched Bobby shuffle up to the door of a huge two story home – his first victim. He stood at the door briefly and was invited inside. Tank was stunned.

Now what do I do. He's inside the home of total strangers – strangers who Bobby had robbed.

After at least ten minutes – that seemed more like an hour to Tank – Bobby came bounding out the door and raced to the car. "Tank ... Tank dey gave me cookies and sumthin called egg noggin ... and I liked it!"

"It's egg nog, Bobby – a popular Christmas drink. What did they say about the things you stole?"

"Sumthin about 'it was juss stuff an dat people are more important than stuff.' I never heard it put like dat b'fer."

"They're right, and we need to talk about the importance of priorities, but first let's finish this job. Don't expect everyone to be as nice as the first stop."

Tank was right. At the remaining homes Bobby visited, the responses ranged from angry words to tearful hugs. After the last of the stolen goods was returned to its rightful owner, Tank took his new little friend to the Grand Coney – for lunch. Bobby ate as much as Tank.

While they were devouring their lunch, Tank brought up the subject of names. "Bobby, I don't think you know about how many famous men went by your name. They've been leaders in most sports, politics, music –

you name it ... there's a popular Bobby there. Today, a world-famous cook is Bobby Flay. The current governor of Louisiana is Bobby Jindal. I'm sure if we Googled it we could find many important men named Bobby. Someday your name could be added to that list."

"You really think so, Tank?"

"Yes, I do but it won't be easy. I think ... what you did today can be a great start."

Back at Bobby's humble home, Tank pulled out a twenty dollar bill and handed it across the seat to his passenger.

"Why don't you use this to get a few groceries? It's not much, but it may help. Let's get together again soon. I'm in the Ravines Apartments – here's my cell number."

~

Entering his den, Pete found Phil relaxing in the Lazy Boy – engrossed in the Grand Rapids Press. Glancing up from the paper, he saw a big grin on Pete's face.

"Was the funeral that entertaining?"

Pete chuckled "I did have trouble keeping my composure when they had several attendees stand and give tributes to the deceased. They had a hard time keeping a solemn tone to the occasion. But, afterwards, I met someone ... someone, I think, I would like to get to know better."

~ Chapter Thirty-One ~

Before Pete could remove his coat and boots, Phil tossed aside the paper. “Okay, Romeo, I can tell by that silly grin that this ‘someone’ is a lady! Speak up! Let’s hear it, and I want all the juicy details!”

“Whoa, boy! Let me, at least, get comfortable.”

“I don’t remember ever seeing you more comfortable – if your face says anything about comfort, that is.” Slipping out of Pete’s recliner, he continued “But ... maybe you need your favorite chair so you can relax and tell your friend all about your next conquest.”

“Is that what you think about my miserable unsuccessful search for the lady of my dreams?”

“So, you’ve been dreaming about some special lady?”

“Well, it’s been on my mind a lot lately ... especially since a few failed attempts. There just has to be someone out there for me. Maybe she’s the one.”

“Okay, Pete enough preliminaries, let’s hear it!”

“YES, SIR. As I was leaving the main sanctuary of my church, I saw a friend from another church where Julie and I had been members. She was with her elderly father and an attractive younger gal, whom I didn’t recognize.”

“So, you went right up and introduced yourself, right?”

“No, I asked my friend, Margaret, about her and she told me that she was her younger sister, Ruth.”

“Then you asked for her phone number, didn’t you?”

"No, but I did whisper 'She's cute, Maggie.' She simply told me that I should ask her out."

"Did you?"

"Not that suddenly ... but I did notice a sweet – beautiful smile from her as I passed them in the parking lot. We'll have to see what develops in the next week or so."

"So, are you going to leave this opportunity to chance, Pete? That doesn't sound like you."

"Maybe I'm learning to be a little more patient. Being in a hurry certainly hasn't worked that well for me."

Pete picked up the sports section of the Press and Phil got the signal that their conversation was now complete.

~

A few days later, Pete received a call from Maggie. She was adamant that Pete should call Ruth and, practically, guaranteed him that she would accept his invitation to a meal in a nearby restaurant.

When Pete made the call, he got the impression that Ruth was expecting to hear from him. *Was Maggie playing the role of cupid? Had she told Ruth to expect my call? Guess it doesn't matter. She seems pleased and wants to meet me!*

They met for dinner at one of Ruth's favorite restaurants, which was just a short drive for both of them. Pete sensed that Ruth was slightly uncomfortable – as was he. As they talked over the meal, they soon learned that they were both carrying some 'excess baggage' from the past.

Ruth had experienced some awful mistreatment over the years and was dealing with a beaten down self-image. Pete was dealing with grief, loneliness and rejection. It seemed like they were meant for each other. They both agreed that the past was history and decided to move forward, not looking back, and to meet again.

They were soon dating frequently and time seemed to fly by. After about three months, they became engaged and chose July 16, 2011 for their wedding date. It was a very small private ceremony. This time no one backed out.

~

During the six months that Ruth and Pete were enjoying most of their time together, Phil had completed his stint as Wysocki's teaching assistant and was within weeks of completing his doctoral requirements. He had arranged to move into the faculty housing in early May, after classes were finished for the term and lodging was available.

Tank and Tiny had become Phil's star pupils and had volunteered to help him move again – without being asked. They were also spending a couple hours a week, between spring practices, with Bobby ... who now was proudly wearing his given name.

Tank was testing his communication skills on Tiny and Bobby. He was determined to teach them to use proper grammar and get rid of their lazy tongues. He wasn't sure which of his two 'students' was showing the most progress. From day to day, it seemed to change. He decided the competition was a good thing.

Bobby asked the owners of the building where he lived if they would pay him to clean up the back alley and do some handiwork. They agreed to a wage and told him they would deduct his pay from his mom's monthly rent. He also got a paper route and decided to try school again. This time he had a new purpose – to be the next famous 'Bobby.' Oh, yes, about that new paper route. You'll never guess who some of his customers are.

~

Back at Pete's condo, one day during all the flurry of activity, Phil confronted him and asked if they could go to dinner and spend a couple hours and just chat a bit.

Pete's mind started to conjure up all sorts of questions ... *Now what does he want? Is he going to quiz me about my spiritual life? Is he concerned about Ruth and me? Is it about his moving out? Does he need help? I guess the only way to find out is to let him tell me.*

So, Pete agreed to go to supper with him on a night that Ruth was busy helping her father.

After they had placed their order, Phil spoke up. "I think you know what I'm going to ask, Pete, so I'll get right to the point. What have you done to reconnect spiritually?"

"First of all ... thanks for your concern and persistence. You'll be pleased to know that Ruth and I are attending church regularly and we've joined a weeknight Bible study. She's been a REAL BLESSING for me, Phil!"

That's great, Pete! I hope my moving out doesn't cause us to lose contact. We've become such good friends."

~ Chapter Thirty-Two ~

One evening, as their spring term was about to end, the faculty and staff of Grand Valley staged an extravagant retirement party for their long-time professor and friend, Peter Daniels, PhD. Everyone was invited and, from the size of the crowd, Pete suspected everyone came.

His soon to be former boarder, Phil, called him aside and asked about Pete's next big event – the wedding. They had both been so busy that their chat times seemed to be a thing of the past.

"About your wedding" he whispered "do you need a best man? If so I'm available and you know how much I like wedding cake, right?"

Somewhat surprised at the question and its timing, Pete tactfully advised him "I'm sorry; I should have told you that my new brother-in-law is going to be my best man. Ruth's sister, will be her maid of honor. The only other people will be Ruth's dad and the preacher."

"That's all ... six people ... no family?"

"Yes, but the next day, that's Saturday afternoon, we are inviting our family and friends to an open house at our community lodge. We definitely want you to be there."

"I wouldn't miss it!"

When the big day arrived, Phil had moved out, but he was at the open house as promised. This was the last time Pete saw him until fall.

~

Pete and Ruth had been married about two months, when Phil called one day hinting that he'd like to meet Pete for lunch. "How about the Grand Coney – say about 11:45?"

Pete agreed and met him at the door.

Phil picked the old pro's brain, throughout the meal, seeking advice concerning his new position as a teaching fellow. Then leaning back in his chair, he sighed and said "So how's married life treating you, Pete?"

Looking around at the nearby tables and leaning in with his elbows on the table he folded his hands "I was hoping you wouldn't ask ..."

"I don't want to probe, Pete ... troubles?"

"I guess not any more than any new marriage."

"What's the problem?"

"It seems we have some major differences in taste."

"You mean like food preferences?"

"No ... that would be an easy fix."

"What then?"

"I like simple ... just like Julie did. She likes busy ... rock gardens in the yard, pictures, plaques, plants ... frills all over the place. I feel like it's closing in on me."

"Are you claustrophobic?"

"Not that I know of, but it's entirely my own fault."

"How so, Pete?"

“I told her if we could stay in my place she could make it her own ... and she did!”

Phil, being single all of his life, simply grinned and said “I’ve read about times of adjustment. It sounds like you have entered those times. Most of my studies on marital adjustments advise calm, loving, direct communication.”

“We do love each other and we are working our way through this. It’s just a matter of time.”

“Yes, Pete, time and communication ... time alone won’t solve anything. Neglected wounds fester. Let’s plan to get together again soon to talk more.”

“Sounds good! Maybe I should have spent more time in psychology studies – I would be better able to cope.”

“Isn’t there a saying that someone who serves as his own shrink has a fool for both counselor and patient?”

On that note, they each went back to their busy lives.

~

In spite of good intentions, Pete and Phil didn’t have their next talk until much later. Knowing that Phil would be staying in town for the holidays, Ruth suggested they invite him over for Christmas day. After a satisfying meal, Pete nodded in the direction of the den. Following him, Phil stopped and looked around in obvious delight. “Hmm ...it looks a bit different in here.”

“Yeah, and I’m okay with it now.”

“That’s better than our last conversation. You know, we never did talk about your nicknames on campus.”

“That’s all water under the bridge now, but I’ve spent my entire life wondering why my parents gave me the first name of a man who DENIED Christ and the middle name of a man who is remembered – even today – as a DOUBTER. Why didn’t they just name me Judas?”

“Don’t forget – those were mistakes they made early in their lives. Later, they became great witnesses ... and your last name is very close to a great Bible prophet.”

“Good point, Phil. You probably noticed last time we met, I was still operating under the crazy notion that I was some sort of knight in shining armor. You know ... the good guy in the white hat ... riding my white horse into town to save the day. I was SO wrong.”

“Confession is good for the soul, friend.”

“We’ve had some heart to heart talks and are committed to having a Christ-centered home. I’ve known all along that salvation is a one-time decision, but I’m learning that our Christian walk is a daily discipline. But it’s not following an impersonal system of legalistic, oppressive, unrealistic and condemning rules. It’s walking with the God of creation, the God of grace and mercy, the loving Lord of glory. It’s trusting in Jesus, who lived a sinless life, died as a sacrifice for sins and rose triumphantly. Oh yeah, and He’s coming soon! It is SO GOOD to be back!

“You know, my friend, you have quite a story. You should write a book.”

“It’s interesting you should mention that. I’ve started pulling my thoughts together and plan to begin writing next month. It’s going to be my life story.”

“Memoirs? Do you think it’ll sell, Pete?”

“We’ll see, my friend, we’ll see ... I hope so!”

~ Clarifications ~

~ To Set the Record Straight ~

Recently, I read a quote attributed to Abraham Lincoln. It went something like this:

I don't read fiction because it's just a bunch of lies.

I didn't use quotation marks because I'm not certain of the exact wording – but you get the general idea. Lies may be a rather harsh word for a Christian book ... but you might say that it's in the Bible. So are some other words I don't feel at liberty to use. Let's just say that, in fiction, sometimes we need to reshape the truth to fit the story. From reading fiction, we have learned to accept this little twist. That being said, please let me explain a few inclusions in my little book.

As I mentioned in my introduction, (Dear Reader) this is my first attempt at fiction. Those who know better than I, tell us that many fiction writers, especially first timers, include people and places from their own life as models from which they form their characters. I was surprised to learn that Charles Schulz, tremendously popular creator of the Peanuts comic strip, did this very successfully – even using their actual first names.

I have included, and embellished, some real people and events, as well as I can remember them. In each case, a fictitious name was assigned or no name was used. There is one exception and you know who you are, David. If anyone thinks that I have falsely represented them or the event involved – please remember it's just fiction.

Now then, let's get to the nitty-gritty – some specifics.

The Cast of Characters in *Beyond the Sunset*

Julie is the name I gave my first wife, Jane, who is now with the Lord. Everything I said about her is true. She was all of that and more – no embellishment was needed. Rest in peace, dear friend.

Ruth is the name my new wife, Karen, selected. She was one of my proofreaders and seemed comfortable with the way she was depicted. She is now my true love and a daily blessing. Most marriages have time of adjustments. Ours was no exception.

Pete is me. I know, he was much better educated than I am, but that is part of shaping the facts to fit the story. Imagine that, I'm a doctor of philosophy, who would have guessed? Not my instructors. Most of my growing up story and the events around, and after, Jane's death are presented as accurately as I could recall them. I don't recall any serious doubt issues – just the grief.

Pete's family is my family, represented quite accurately. I did make some juicy modifications. They're a great bunch. Those of you who know them can attest to that.

Pete's parents are a quite truly represented. They were a genuine demonstration of God's grace once they submitted to His direction.

Pete's grandfather never admitted to any need for help. He died a lonely, miserable old drunk ... without Christ – without hope.

Pete's sweetheart across town was a really sweet girl. She and her amazing family left an impression on me, as a brash young lad, that I still cherish today. It was a real pleasure to meet her and her fine husband some months ago. They have two grown kids including a son who is a pastor. That's cool!

Pete's other 103 girls on his list before meeting Jane If you're just learning about the list, I'm sorry. What can I say? I was just a kid. Now, as an old guy, I couldn't name many of you. Recently, a gal I dated twice, told me that she didn't even remember it. Humph ... some impression I made.

The ladies Pete dated after Jane's passing only a few of you are mentioned in my story. If you weren't, you're probably relieved. To those who were, you may remember things differently. Maybe I fabricated a bit. To all of you ... thanks for your help and understanding in some difficult times. Any one of you could make some guy a fine wife.

Don who consoled me the day after Jane's passing is a real person – as real as you can find. He and Connie are some of the finest people I've known. They're pretty good golfers too.

Phil, Tank, Tiny, Doctor Wysocki, Chig/Bobby are some of my imaginary friends. There are others in this book who play minor roles. I know that I'm too old to have imaginary friends. But when they wake me up in the middle of the night to write about them, what else can I do?

Charles Schulz is someone everyone knew, except Tiny. So his infatuation with the little red-haired girl apparently didn't come from Peanuts.

The places mentioned in __*Beyond the Sunset*__

Grand Valley State University has several locations. The campus where this story, supposedly takes place is in Allendale, Michigan. My only visits to this property were online. This book is fiction. Nothing mentioned herein really happened there. Their website is filled with information, including an excellent map of the campus. After much reading, I can assure you that their security record is nothing short of amazing. I seriously doubt any theft like I feature could ever happen there.

McDonalds in Allendale has a friendly staff. The quarter coffee is only available to fictitious characters.

Grand Coney is a nice homey place to get some great hot dogs and many other tasty features. I can vouch for that – I've been there a few times.

Los Aztecas Mexican Restaurant was in operation when my characters went there. Unfortunately, it burned down June 12, 2012.

Manny's Café and Valleyview Church are figments of my imagination. You can search high and low throughout all of Allendale – but you won't find them. Sorry!

Ruth's Chris Steak House is an upscale place to go for your very special occasions ... especially if your budget is like mine. I've been to the one in Saint Louis. If enough people buy my book, I would like to try the one in Grand Rapids.

Thanks to all who played a role in this book – real and imaginary. I couldn't have done it without you.

Some of the books I've read while writing

Beyond the Sunset

The Adjustable Halo by Ken Anderson
(Word Books, Publishers 1968)

Answers to Tough Questions by Josh McDowell and Don Stewart
Here's Life Publishers, Inc. 1980)

Case for Christ by Lee Strobel (Zondervan 2005)

Case for the Real Jesus by Lee Strobel (Zondervan 2007)

Cosmos, Creator and Human Destiny: Answering Darwin, Dawkins and the New Atheists by Dave Hunt (Berean Call 2010)

Evidence That Demands a Verdict by Josh McDowell
(Campus Crusade for Christ 1972)

Finding God at Harvard compiled and edited by Kelly Monroe
(Zondervan Publishing House 1996)

He Who Thinks Has To Believe by A. E. Wilder-Smith
(Master Books a Division of CLP Publishers 1981)

Hellbent for Election by P. Speshock
(Zondervan Publishing House 1964)

Inside One Author's Heart by Eugenia Price (Doubleday 1992)

Jack's Story: The Life Story of C. S. Lewis by Douglas Gresham
(Broadman and Holman Publishers 2005)

Know What You Believe by Paul E. Little (IVP Books 2008)

Know Why You Believe by Paul E. Little (IVP Books 2008)

Mere Christianity by C. S. Lewis (Harper Collins Publishers 1980)

O Love That Will Not Let Me Go: Facing Death with Courageous Confidence in God edited by Nancy Guthrie
(Crossway 2011)

Screwtape Letters by C. S. Lewis (Harper Collins Publishers 2001

Seven Reasons Why a Scientist Believes in God by A. Cressy Morrison (Fleming H. Revell Company 1962)

A Shepherd Looks at Psalm 23 by Phillip Keller (Zondervan Publishing House 1970)

Skeptics Answered by D. James Kennedy (Multnomah Books 1997)

Unconditional by Eva Marie Everson (Broadman and Holman Publishers 2012)

Understanding the Times by David A. Noebel (Summit Ministries 1991 Harvest House Publishers)

What's So Great about Christianity by Dinesh D'Sousa (Tyndale House Publishers 2007)

Who Moved the Stone? by Frank Morrison (Zondervan Publishing House 1977)

Wrecked: When a Broken World Slams into Your Comfortable Life by Jeff Goings (Moody Publishers 2012)

Writing for the Soul by Jerry B. Jenkins (Writer's Digest Books 2006)

Your God is Too Small by J. B. Phillips (Simon and Schuster, Inc. 2004)

The most important book, the Bible, is as essential to spiritual growth as food is to physical growth. Devotional reading and intense study are vital. I own many translations and paraphrases and enjoy consulting all of them.

My previous writing includes various training manuals, promotional literature and newsletter articles. This is my first attempt at fiction, so I've also read many "how to" books. Then, I did it my way. Don't blame the experts ... I take full responsibility for my obstinacy and the results. A number of the above titles I had read many years some time ago but considered them worthy of reading again.

Songs and Hymns that helped me through the most difficult days ...

Speaking to yourselves in Psalms, Hymns and spiritual songs, singing and making melody in your heart to the Lord Ephesians 5:19

There are thousands of wonderful songs and hymns. Here are a few that helped me in my grieving process and still bless my life today. Don't let the song go out of your heart!

Amazing Grace

Amazing Grace, how sweet the sound,
That saved a wretch like me!
I once was lost but now am found,
Was blind, but now I see.

T'was Grace that taught
My heart to fear,
And Grace, my fears relieved;
How precious did that Grace appear
The hour I first believed!

Through many dangers, toils and snares
I have already come;
T'was Grace that brought me safe thus far,
And Grace will lead us home.

The Lord has promised good to me
His word my hope secures.
He will my shield and portion be,
As long as life endures.

When we've been here ten thousand years,
Bright shining as the sun,
We've no less days to sing God's praise
Than when we've first begun.

John Newton

Because He Lives

God sent His Son, they called Him Jesus
He came to love, heal, and forgive
He lived and died to buy my pardon
An empty grave is there to prove
my Saviour lives.

Chorus
Because He lives I can face tomorrow
Because He lives all fear is gone
Because I know He holds the future
And life is worth the living
just because He lives.

How sweet to hold a new born baby
And feel the pride, a joy he gives
But greater still the calm assurance
This child can face uncertain days
because He lives.
And then one day I'll cross the river
I'll fight life's final war with pain
And then as death gives way to vict'ry
I'll see the lights of glory and
I'll know He lives.

Words by William J. and Gloria Gaither
Music by William J. Gaither

Beyond the Sunset

Beyond the sunset, O blissful morning
When with our Saviour heaven is begun
Earth's toiling ended, O glorious dawning
Beyond the sunset when day is done.

Beyond the sunset, no clouds will gather
No storms will threaten, no fears annoy
O day of gladness, O day unending
Beyond the sunset eternal joy.

Beyond the sunset, a hand will guide me
To God the Father whom I adore
His glorious presence, His words of welcome
Will be my portion on that fair shore.

Beyond the sunset, O glad reunion
With our dear loved ones who've gone before
In that fair homeland we'll know no parting
Beyond the sunset forever more...

Virgil and Blanche Kerr Brock

Day by Day

Day by day, and with each passing moment,
Strength I find, to meet my trials here;
Trusting in my Father's wise bestowment,
I've no cause for worry or for fear.
He Whose heart is kind beyond all measure
Gives unto each day what He deems best—
Lovingly, it's part of pain and pleasure,
Mingling toil with peace and rest.

Every day, the Lord Himself is near me
With a special mercy for each hour;
All my cares He fain would bear and cheer me,
He Whose Name is Counselor and Power;
The protection of His child and treasure
Is a charge that on Himself He laid;
As thy days, thy strength shall be in measure,
This the pledge to me He made.

Help me then in every tribulation
So to trust Thy promises, O Lord,
That I lose not faith's sweet consolation
Offered me within Thy holy Word.
Help me, Lord, when toil and trouble meeting,
E'er to take, as from a father's hand,
One by one, the days, the moments fleeting,
Till I reach the promised land.

Karolina Wilhelmina Sandell Berg

God Will Take Care of You

**Be not dismayed whate'er betide,
God will take care of you;
Beneath His wings of love abide,
God will take care of you.**

**Chorus
God will take care of you,
Through every day, o'er all the way;
He will take care of you,
God will take care of you.**

**Through days of toil when heart doth fail,
God will take care of you;
When dangers fierce your path assail,
God will take care of you.**

**All you may need He will provide,
God will take care of you;
Nothing you ask will be denied,
God will take care of you.**

**No matter what may be the test,
God will take care of you;
Lean, weary one, upon His breast,
God will take care of you.**

Civilla Durfee Martin
Public domain

Living for Jesus

**Living for Jesus, a life that is true,
Striving to please Him in all that I do;
Yielding allegiance, glad hearted and free,
This is the pathway of blessing for me.**

**Chorus
Jesus, Lord and Savior, I give myself to Thee,
For Thou, in Thy atonement,
didst give Thyself for me.
I own no other Master;
my heart shall be Thy throne.
My life I give, henceforth to live,
O Christ, for Thee alone.**

**Living for Jesus Who died in my place,
Bearing on Calvary my sin and disgrace;
Such love constrains me to answer His call,
Follow His leading and give Him my all.**

**Living for Jesus, wherever I am,
Doing each duty in His holy Name;
Willing to suffer affliction and loss,
deeming each trial a part of my cross.**

**Living for Jesus through earth's little while,
My dearest treasure, the light of His smile;
Seeking the lost ones He died to redeem,
Bringing the weary to find rest in Him.**

Thomas O. Chisholm
Public domain

Moment by Moment

Dying with Jesus, by death reckoned mine;
Living with Jesus, a new life divine;
Looking to Jesus till glory doth shine,
Moment by moment, O Lord, I am Thine.

Chorus
Moment by moment I'm kept in His love;
Moment by moment I've life from above;
Looking to Jesus till glory doth shine;
Moment by moment, O Lord, I am Thine.

Never a trial that He is not there,
Never a burden that He doth not bear,
Never a sorrow that He doth not share,
Moment by moment, I'm under His care.

Never a heartache, and never a groan,
Never a teardrop, and never a moan;
Never a danger but there on the throne,
Moment by moment He thinks of His own.

Never a weakness that He doth not feel,
Never a sickness that He cannot heal;
Moment by moment, in woe or in weal,
Jesus my Savior abides with me still.

Daniel W. Whittle
Public domain

One Day He's Coming

One day when Heaven was filled with His praises,
One day when sin was as black as could be;
Jesus came forth to be born of a virgin,
Dwelt among men, my example is He!

Chorus
Living, He loved me,
Dying, He saved me,
Buried, He carried my sins far away;
Rising He justified freely forever:
One day He's coming
Oh glorious day, oh glorious day!

One day they led Him up Calvary's mountain,
One day they nailed Him to die on a tree;
Suffering anguish, despised and rejected,
Bearing our sins, my Redeemer is He!

One day they left Him alone in the garden,
One day He rested from suffering free;
Angels came down o'er His tomb to keep vigil,
Hope of the hopeless, my Savior is He!

One day the grave could conceal Him no longer,
One day the stone rolled away from the door;
Then He arose, over death He had conquered,
Now He's ascended, my Lord evermore!

One day the trumpet will sound for His coming,
One day the skies with His glories will shine;
Wonderful day, my Beloved One, bringing!
Glorious Savior, this Jesus, is mine!

J. Wilbur Chapman Public domain

Rock of Ages

**Rock of Ages, cleft for me,
let me hide myself in thee;
let the water and the blood,
from thy wounded side which flowed,
be of sin the double cure;
save from wrath and make me pure.**

**Not the labors of my hands
can fulfill thy law's commands;
could my zeal no respite know,
could my tears forever flow,
all for sin could not atone;
thou must save, and thou alone.**

**Nothing in my hand I bring,
simply to the cross I cling;
naked, come to thee for dress;
helpless, look to thee for grace;
foul, I to the fountain fly;
wash me, Savior, or I die.**

**While I draw this fleeting breath,
when mine eyes shall close in death,
when I soar to worlds unknown,
see thee on thy judgment throne,
Rock of Ages, cleft for me,
let me hide myself in thee.**

Augustus M. Toplady

What a Friend We Have in Jesus

What a Friend we have in Jesus,
All our sins and griefs to bear!
What a privilege to carry
Everything to God in prayer!
O what peace we often forfeit,
O what needless pain we bear,
All because we do not carry
Everything to God in prayer.

Have we trials and temptations?
Is there trouble anywhere?
We should never be discouraged;
Take it to the Lord in prayer.
Can we find a friend so faithful
Who will all our sorrows share?
Jesus knows our every weakness;
Take it to the Lord in prayer.

Are we weak and heavy laden,
Cumbered with a load of care?
Precious Savior, still our refuge,
Take it to the Lord in prayer.
Do thy friends despise, forsake thee?
Take it to the Lord in prayer!
In His arms He'll take and shield thee;
Thou wilt find a solace there.

Joseph Medlicott Scriven
Public domain

What are some of your Favorites?